Down

The Dark

Path

The Complete Trilogy

A Cheating Wife's Journey

From Innocence to Submission

JJ Stuart

Standard Legal Blurb

Table of Contents

"This Trilogy is dedicated to my Wife, who somehow puts up with me and tolerates the hours I spend crafting erotic stories. You are awesome babe, and you look good in soft light too!"

JJ Stuart

September 2016

My alarm clock went off, snapping me out of my dream where I was tied to a table while tanned muscular men, kissed and caressed my naked flesh. But I wasn't on a table. I was in my bed. I stared at the ceiling fan in the early morning light and listened to the soft static of what was supposed to be the morning news and weather. Someone must have been playing with the dials again. My son, no doubt. I just needed five more minutes in that dream. *Damn.*

I glanced at my snoring husband and sighed. Reaching up, I flipped off my radio and contemplated reasons to call in sick today. I had a class of rowdy grade nine students for English first thing and then two periods of story composition with my undisciplined grade tens. My students needed me, though, so I abandoned reasons to call in sick and rolled out of bed. Grabbing my housecoat, I slipped it on and checked on my three-year-old son. He was sleeping soundly which made me happy. Stifling a yawn, I trudged towards the bathroom to take a shower.

Lately, my little son was the only person that seemed to make me happy. I wouldn't say my marriage was on the rocks, but it could use some spice; perhaps a whole bottle of it. I love my little family, but in my mind's eye, I could see my future locked in a dreary routine. A routine of waking up each morning, then getting my son ready and making lunches before I drop junior off at daycare, and then rush to school so I could teach other parent's kids all day. After school I would pick up junior from daycare, then rush home to make supper and clean up, while also making sure the laundry is done. If I'm lucky, I might get some time to work on lesson plans until I bath junior and put him to bed. Then more cleaning and maybe, if I'm really lucky, catch a little television before I go to bed exhausted, ready to repeat the process again the next day.

I know I have a responsibility as a parent, but I feel that if I don't get things done around the house, then they won't get done at all. Responsibility though, needs to be shared. I wish my husband would get up with me in the morning and help with the chores. I wish I came home from work to a dinner already made instead of having to make it myself. Just once I'd like to see the laundry folded and put away without me having to do it. It seems everybody puts demands on my time, and sometimes I wonder when I will ever get time for myself.

I turned the shower on, dropped my robe and peered in the mirror. I saw a tired twenty-four-year-old housewife and mother staring back at me. Gone was the goody-two-shoes teenager with dreams and ambitions. I did what everyone said and got my teaching degree and then a job at a good school. I married my high school sweetheart and started a family. Hell, I even had a white picket fence. I did everything right. So why was I unhappy? Routine. Soul sucking routine. I felt like I was trapped in a very small box with nothing to carry me into old age except weariness and repetition.

One day I'd wake up with gray hair and look back with regret that I lived my whole life for others and forgot to have fun along the way. Logic said I should be happy, but in my heart, I was miserable. I needed something to revive my soul. I needed to feel young at heart again, not burdened with endless demands with no relief and no help and no end in sight.

After my shower, I woke junior and fed him breakfast. While he made a trail of Cheerios across the table, I made lunches. I noticed the pile of dirty laundry and added it to my list of things to get done later. I debated waking my husband, but what's the point? Tim gets so grumpy in the morning, and I didn't want him yelling at our little monkey for making a Cheerio mess on the table. I'll just do everything myself – as usual.

I dressed in a smart white blouse and navy blue skirt. My legs needed shaving, so I covered them with nylons. Shaving my legs was just one more thing to add to my list. Once junior was dressed, we slipped out the door, and into the van. As I pulled out of the driveway, I looked back at our house and knew my husband hadn't even woken yet. Must be nice to sleep in every day.

With a dreary hand on the steering wheel, I dropped monkey off at daycare and hurried to school. I dreaded facing my grade nine class, but there is nothing I could do. It's my job, so I sucked it up. I put on a fake smile and pretended I have my shit together.

The one bright spot in my day is Brad. He's a fellow teacher in the English department who's a little shy and more than a little odd. He greets me every morning with a cheerful hello and some quirky comment about some random factoid or thought on his mind. He never fails to put a smile on my face.

I saw Brad getting out of his little red car when I pulled into the teacher's parking lot. I wheeled my van around and parked beside him as he looked up in surprise and gave me a big wave. For some reason, he is wearing a plaid shirt, beige cargo pants, hushpuppies and a bright lime green tie that makes my eyes hurt. He's such a dork, but he's an adorable dork.

"Good morning, Julie. Did you know if you add three packages of sweetener instead of sugar to your coffee, without knowing it, you get one heck of a shock?"

I smile in the early morning sunshine while I shoulder my bag and lock my van. "Let me guess," I ask while shutting my door, "you had a rough morning?"

"To put it mildly, yes. I hadn't realized my blunder until I was on the road and took a big gulp. Care to try? It's awful." He offered me his travel mug.

"I'm more of a tea drinker," I say and feel my spirits rise for the first time today. As he comes closer, I shield my eyes in pretend agony. "What's with the tie?"

"Oh, this." He looked down sheepishly. "I thought it was a different color when I got dressed this morning. Apparently, don't have see-in-the-dark super powers because I could have sworn it was beige. Pretend for me and everything will be fine."

I can't help but laugh. "Okay, if anyone asks, I'll cover for you."

"Appreciated. Hey, you have plans for lunch?"

"Hum, marking papers probably. Why?"

"I need to find a good sandwich shop."

He is amusing if anything, so I press him for details. "Do I even want to know why you need a sandwich shop?"

"I have a craving for corn beef," Brad paused to open the staff entrance door for me. "Want to come help me sample different places?"

I step into the school, smiling as he holds the door. His tie really is terrible up close. I glanced down the hallway and see students milling around their lockers waiting for first period to start. Even though it's only early September, I can tell it's going to be a hectic day.

"I don't think we have time to hit many sandwich shops," I said over my shoulder while adjusting my bag. Brad catches up. "There can't be very many in the city."

"Well, we won't know unless we try. How about we hit one deli a day until I find the perfect corn beef sandwich? It could be a quest."

I look at him again. "So is this a fancy way of asking me out on a date?"

"If it was, would there be kissing?"

"Definitely not," I scold him in a mocking tone. I love his humor.

"Good then, consider it a date. I didn't want to kiss you anyway."

I slapped his arm gently. "I'm very kissable, thank you very much." We stopped outside my English class. I can see some of the bratty kids inside, and my heart sinks. Just one period, I tell myself.

"Besides, you aren't my type," Brad continued matter-of-factly. When he saw me open my classroom door, he looked confused. "Aren't you going to the English office first?"

"No, not today. I have to set up a projector. Catch you at lunch. No kissing."

"It's a date. Hey, are you sure you don't want my coffee?"

"I'm sure, Brad. Now go," I said with a smile.

He nodded and turned away. I watched him stroll down the hallway, to a chorus of muffled laughter, as students notice his horrible tie. Despite his terrible wardrobe and awkward social graces, I found him attractive. I wouldn't put him in the total hunk category, but he was handsome; maybe a seven out of ten on the hotness scale. I found myself laughing as he started to explain his poor fashion choices to students while he walked. Despite the gloomy start to my day, Brad put me in a good mood. I couldn't help but wonder who even craves corn beef?

By lunch time I was craving corn beef too. I couldn't recall the last time I ate it, and when I bumped into Brad in the staff room, I was ready to order a double decker with a giant dill pickle.

And that was how my relationship with Brad began; searching for corn beef sandwiches during the first weeks of school and telling each other how much we didn't want to kiss. It was perfect.

Every day for the next week Brad and I left the school at lunch in search of the perfect sandwich. Being the dork that he was, Brad had printed a list of every sandwich shop and deli joint in the city. It turned out there were a lot more than I would have guessed.

Each day I laughed and enjoyed myself while eating copious amounts of strange sandwiches and exotic meats at each new place we found. Brad regaled me with quirky stories and funny anecdotes, but he never tried to kiss me. We were both married and kept our relationship as strictly friends. Once I realized he wasn't trying to seduce me, I began to relax and look forward to our little excursions more and more.

My life at home and in my marriage was still dreary and predictable, but at least I had this one social outlet to help me feel youthful again. Brad didn't know it, but he had lifted me out of a dark place, and I appreciated him for it.

After the last sandwich joint had sadly been crossed off our list, Brad took me to a coffee shop where we sat down and debated who had the best sandwiches. I don't remember ever laughing so hard in all my life. He was certain a little deli near the airport served the best sandwich while I preferred the vegetarian place downtown. Brad was offended by the very notion that a vegetarian sandwich shop would serve fake corn beef substitute. But I liked it.

We eventually decided to call our argument a draw. I would continue to get my vegetarian sandwiches while he would get his deli favorite by the airport. As we drove back to class, Brad asked me out-of-the-blue if he could send me emails.

"Of course, you can. What a silly question," I said.

"Are you sure your husband won't mind?"

"Why would he mind? I get work emails all the time at home."

"I just want to be sure. Do you have an instant chat?"

I had to think for a moment while I drove. "No, but I can download one if you want. Why? Do you need to chat with me tonight?"

"I have ideas for the English department. I want to bounce them off you outside of official channels, if you know what I mean."

I knew what he meant. All of our official work emails were monitored and read by the school board. He wanted to communicate outside those snooping eyes. It made sense, especially if we were talking smack about other teachers.

"I can't see why not," I said. At the next stoplight, I opened my purse and scribbled my email on a notepad, then tore the sheet off and handed it to Brad. "What chat program would be best?"

"I like Torrid Chat. It's encrypted and never leaves a history."

"I've never heard of Torrid Chat. Is it free?"

"It's free, but if you pay like ten bucks, you won't get any advertisements. I'll email you the link."

"That sounds great," I said. The light turned green.

* * *

That night I got my first email from Brad. I had already bathed and tucked my little prince into bed and was reclining on the couch with my iPad tablet when his email arrived. My husband, Tim, was downstairs like he was every night, playing some shooter game. I could hear the noise through the floor.

I opened my email and clicked on his message:

Here is the link. My username is DarkRyder69. Once your account is set up, send me a friend request. We can chat a little tonight if you want – Brad.

I felt my heart quicken in my chest, and I looked up. Why did I feel naughty? What kind of name was DarkRyder69 anyway? I felt an unfamiliar rush course through my body as I opened the website Brad had given me. I browsed the blurb about how Torrid Chat was designed to facilitate secrecy between consenting adults. There were statistics on cheating and infidelity, and the website boasted its chat program was virtually undetectable to a suspicious spouse. Why did I need this level of secrecy? Then it dawned on me.

Was I having an affair?

I had to think about it. I shook my head, of course not. Brad was just a friend from work who wanted to talk about work stuff. Why he wanted to use this particular chat program instead of the myriad of others available, I didn't know. Perhaps he used that account for years, so it was convenient. Or perhaps his wife had snooped around on his computer, in the past, and he felt the need for privacy. As far as I was concerned, one program was as good as another. If Brad wanted Torrid Chat, then it was fine with me. I doubted we would ever chat much or send many emails to each other anyway.

I downloaded the program. The setup required my username. I paused for a moment, considering my options. I hated making up names. Finally, a name came to me.

GoldenGirl24.

Using a secret email address – that Tim didn't know about – I created my username, and installed the software. After verifying my email address, I was officially a member of Torrid Chat. *Woot!*

I searched for Brad's handle: DarkRyder69. Next, I had to figure out how to add Brad as a friend. After finally discovering it, I wrote an invite message:

GoldenGirl24: Hey, this is Julie. Just for the record vegetarians rule and only dorks eat corn beef sandwiches!

I laughed and pressed send.

Brad replied quickly. He must have been sitting by his computer waiting. I watched as Torrid Chat created a private chat session and we were connected. I moved my laptop to a small coffee table so when my husband comes upstairs, he won't see anything suspicious. Not that I was worried about what my husband thought. I had a plausible excuse for what I was doing. I was only chatting about work with a colleague. Nothing more. Still, it didn't hurt to be cautious.

For the better part of two hours, Brad and I chatted about being school teachers and about life in general. I learned some of his favorite movies and music, while he learned I'm afraid of heights and that sometimes I sing in the shower.

Over the next month, we spent more and more time together between teaching classes at school. Not always, but at least a few times a week, we would visit a sandwich place from our old list and grab a quick lunch together. I guess our friendship grew from there.

At night we bitched about students and other staff members and exchanged jokes and funny memes from the internet. It felt like there was someone out there who truly understood who I was as a woman, and appreciated me. Brad learned about my hopes and fears, and I, in turn, learned about his. We were connecting on an emotional level like best friends.

Meanwhile, my husband continued to stay up late playing video games and sleeping in during the times in the morning when I needed him most. I wouldn't say we were growing distant, but at times I did feel that way. We had our routine; I did everything, and Tim did very little. At least I had Brad to listen to me gripe and complain. He often suggested ideas to spice up my marriage, but they never worked. Twice during our first month of chatting, I took Brad's advice and wore sexy lingerie to bed. My husband never noticed. Either time.

As September rolled into October, I felt more and more like I could tell Brad anything. Each day when I arrived at school, I looked forward to greeting him and listening to his strange anecdotes. Part of me wanted to hug him, but there were too many eyes around the school. Too many staff and students knew both Brad and I were married, and *not* to each other. Being spotted hugging or holding hands was far too risky.

"I wish we could snuggle on the couch and watch a movie," I said to Brad one day while we drove to a deli for lunch.

"I would love that," Brad agreed.

His admission startled me. Snuggling on a couch together was crossing the line, and I didn't know he was actually willing to do such a thing.

"Are you serious?" I asked him.

Brad nodded. "I would love to snuggle with you. My wife and I used to do that years ago, but not anymore. I miss it. I feel comfortable around you. But no kissing. That's gross."

I laughed and left it at that. As time passed, the thought of sneaking off somewhere and snuggling on the couch with Brad, sounded more and more appealing. I didn't confess to Brad that my husband doesn't snuggle with me anymore, or how much I missed it. When Tim and I have sex, which is almost never, he always goes back downstairs to play computer games after instead of holding me. I didn't tell Brad, that most of the time, Tim only shows affection when he wants sex. Once I give in, he goes back to his gaming. It's like I'm just there to please him.

Brad and I chatted well into the November, every night and even on weekends. If I went out with my son or (miracle of miracles) my husband tagged along; I would drop Brad a quick email telling him my plans. When I got home, I would immediately let him know. He would ask how my trip was and what we did, and then a whole slew of interesting questions. I felt like Brad was genuinely interested in my life and what I did. I wished I could have said the same about my husband.

One night Brad and I were complaining about bad movie sequels during our chat ritual, and I decided to ask if he remembered the snuggling conversation we had in the van.

GoldenGirl24: Remember when I said I wished we could snuggle on the couch and watch a movie?

DarkRyder69: Yes.

GoldenGirl24: What if I told you I thought of a way we could do that. If you were still interested that is.

DarkRyder69: I am! But not at school. Too risky.

GoldenGirl24: What if I told you I have a key to a friend's house, and they are away on vacation in Europe for a week?

DarkRyder69: Who takes a vacation for a week?

17

GoldenGirl24: What? Lots of people vacations for a week. Have you never taken a vacation?

DarkRyder69: No. I'm a teacher. I only get summers off.

GoldenGirl24: The point is I have a key to their empty house.

DarkRyder69: Yummy!

GoldenGirl24: I take it that's a yes to snuggles and a movie?

DarkRyder69: I'll bring the popcorn!

I laughed and leaned back against the couch, my laptop balanced across my knees. My heart was racing. I felt like a naive school girl all giddy with excitement over going to the prom with a cute boy. I wasn't able to wipe the smile off my face as we continued to chat for another hour or so. I kept imagining what it would be like to be held in Brad's arms.

It would be heaven.

After I reluctantly ended our chat for the night, I walked down to the basement to give my husband a kiss. I felt so happy I needed to express it. Tim was sitting in his boxers wearing a faded army t-shirt. He was furiously trying to dogfight someone in his online airplane game. I put my arms around his shoulders and leaned in for a kiss.

Tim shirked from my touch. "Not now, Honey, I almost got this bastard."

I stepped back and looked at the screen and then at my husband. I folded my arms and patiently waited. My husband's plane erupted in flames, and he struggled to correct, but it was too late. I watched with an amused smile as his character died.

"God Damnit!"

Whoa, I thought. *It's just a game.*

"I swear those fuckers are hacking," Tim cursed as he slammed a fist on his keyboard. I could see some buttons were missing and wondered how often he slammed his keyboard in anger.

"I just came down to tell you I love you and that I'm having a bath," I said.

"Okay, fine," Tim snapped. "I'm going to blow that guy outta the sky."

"I love you," I said quietly.

"Love you too," he said without looking up.

I waited. Tim didn't even make eye contact, and I watched as he selected another airplane and entered battle. Without saying another word, I turned and went back upstairs. I felt like crying. I drew my bath and added some bubbles because bubbles always make me feel better. Tim was always on that damn computer, and I hated it. At least Brad understood and cared about me.

I undressed and looked at myself in the mirror. I'm a twenty-four-year-old housewife, alone in her marriage. Is marriage simply work, clean, feed everyone, tidy up, and keep quiet? Was it too much to ask a husband to show a little interest in his wife other than when he wanted sex? He could exert a little effort and maybe ask me how my day at work was. Or he could offer to wash the dishes after I made supper. I didn't feel appreciated at all. I didn't know a person could live with someone and yet feel so lonely.

* * *

The next morning, I had shaken off my blues and was determined to enjoy my day. Leaving my snoring husband in bed once more, I took our baby monkey to daycare, grabbed an herbal tea from the local drive-thru and scooted to work. Brad was already there, and I parked my van beside his little red car.

It was turning into a beautiful fall day. I always loved watching the leaves change and feel the crispness of the morning air. For some reason, the turning of the trees always made me feel romantic. I couldn't wait to break out my soft sweaters, cashmere turtlenecks, and stylish boots. I wondered if I could persuade Brad to sneak away with me for a romantic walk through the woods when the fall colors came. The thought of that put a smile on my face. I walked into the school deciding I would not let the grade nine English class put a dent in my spirit.

The English office was empty of teachers except for Brad who was sitting at his desk flipping through paperwork. He looked at me and smiled. It was nearly time for class, and I wondered if Brad hung back just to see me. I hope he had.

"Well, isn't that a lovely sight." Brad said.

I flashed him a smile but didn't say anything. I set my tea and purse on my desk and glanced at my cubbyhole mailbox mounted alongside every other teacher's mailbox along the wall. It was empty.

He put his papers down. "Why are you so happy today, Darling?"

My heart skipped a beat. *Did Brad just call me Darling? He did!* My heart warmed at hearing him use such an endearing name for me. I shrugged and said, "I dunno."

I walked over to his desk. When he stood, I gave him a hug and a quick kiss on the cheek. It was his turn to be surprised.

"It's my tie, isn't it?" he said. "You can't resist the tie."

I laughed. "I adore you."

"Really? What did I do to deserve that? It's not every day a beautiful woman strolls into my office with such radiance and plants a kiss on my cheek."

"I'm just happy. Can't a girl be happy without raising suspicions?"

"I suppose so. Did you know if you spit gum out the window while driving, there is a ninety-four percent chance it'll be sucked in your back window?"

His sudden change of topic threw me off for a moment. I was used to Brad suddenly veering off into strange topics, but this wasn't one of those times. Perhaps it was a symptom of nervousness? I recovered, though, and wondered where he got those odd tidbits of information.

"Did you find gum on the back window?" I asked. I wanted to take the conversation back to me being happy.

"Yes. If you spit gum out of the window while you drive, it will come back inside and stick to the most inopportune spot. Such as the headrest."

"Ninety-four percent chance huh? I didn't know that."

"I made that part up to sound more impressive. So, are we on for lunch?"

I pulled a key out of my pocket and dangled it before his eyes.

"Your friend's house key?"

I nodded and gave him a mischievous grin. "How about we snuggle a little?"

Brad rubbed his chin thoughtfully. "We won't have enough time to watch a whole movie before we have to get back."

"I'm not interested in the movie part, you dork. We can pause a movie anyway and watch it in parts," I explained. "Not that I plan on watching much of it."

"That means more snuggling. Hum, I think I like the way you think."

I leaned closer and kissed him on the lips, then turned and dropped the key in my pocket. "You said *think*, twice in a sentence. We're English teachers, and that's a huge turnoff. Sorry, the date's canceled."

His eyes bulged. "My apologies! I seem to be off my game today. I wonder what could have caused that to happen?"

I didn't want him to see my cheeks flushing like some nervous girl, so I turned towards my desk. I picked up my tea in one hand and my teaching notes in the other and then strode towards the door. Stopping in the doorway, I flung my long dark hair over my shoulder like a movie star and fixed Brad with a pouty stare. He was standing and watching me, with an amused smile on his face. I winked, flipped my hair again, and walked to class without glancing back. We had never kissed before, and I thought it best to leave him with a little something to occupy his mind until lunch time.

I relished that stolen kiss all morning and found focusing on teaching to be somewhat difficult. Whenever there was a pause in anything I was working on, my mind replayed the feel of Brad's warm lips. By the time the lunch bell rang, my juices were flowing with anticipation, and my heart was fluttering with nerves. Snuggling on the couch was a huge step for both of us, just like kissing was, and I felt exhilarated.

Brad was waiting for me in the English office with a barely contained grin on his face. I dropped my armload of teaching materials on my desk, scooped my keys, glanced at my empty cubbyhole mailbox, all before giving Brad a raised eyebrow and a nod towards the door. He fell into step without saying a word.

Outside in the bright, crisp air, I glanced at Brad and asked, "So, how was your morning?"

"Distracting."

"Oh, how come?" I asked in an amused voice.

"I was kissed by a beautiful woman this morning, and my brain short-circuited. I haven't been the same since."

"Oh no! Are you seeing another woman behind my back?" I teased.

"I wouldn't dream of it. Actually, I did. But she wasn't as hot as you."

"You better not." I unlocked the van and climbed in. Brad veered around to the passenger side.

The drive to my friend's house was a less than ten minutes long. For students, lunch was seventy-five minutes, but for teachers, it was barely an hour, if they were lucky. Teachers had to be in the classroom ready to start once lunch was over. I had done the arithmetic in my head and figured Brad and I could snuggle for half an hour on the couch. We would still have enough time to get back to school, gobble something down, and make it to class ready to teach.

Stephanie, my vacationing friend, lived in a three story home smack dab in the middle of a growing subdivision. The property was dotted with newly transplanted trees and meticulously manicured flowerbeds tucked away for the coming winter. The driveway was empty as I pulled into it and shut the van off. I felt nervous and hoped none of her neighbors decided to report two people sneaking into a house that wasn't theirs.

"Well, this is it. What do ya think?" I said.

He peered out the van window and whistled. "Looks expensive."

"Her husband is a doctor. She married money. Come on let's go inside. I'll give you the tour," I said as I climbed out.

Brad followed me up the front steps and waited as I unlocked the door. Stepping inside, we saw a spacious foyer covered in rich marble leading to a wide spiral staircase. Expensive art hung on the walls and two finely sculpted cherubim angels guarded the bottom of the staircase.

"Wow, this is nice," Brad observed. "I should have married a doctor."

I wasn't in the mood to admire the expensive home we were commandeering. I slipped my arms around Brad and snuggled into his neck. He wrapped his arms around me and we stood in the stillness of the house and enjoyed each other's company. *Alone at last.*

I shut the front door with my foot, not willing to break our embrace. For long moments we stood in each other's arms. Finally, Brad stepped back and cleared his throat.

"Should we find the living room?"

I brushed some strands of hair from my eyes and nodded. I'd been inside Stephanie's house many times and knew where to go. I lead Brad through the kitchen and towards the back of the house. A large flat screen television and rows of expensive leather couches greeted us as we entered the living room.

"Wow, this is nice," Brad said admiring the décor. He glanced at the television. "Do you know how to work that?"

"I do. Are you going to stand there or spend some quality time with me?"

Brad turned. I was sitting on the couch and patted the cushion beside me. He smiled and joined me. For a moment I felt like a giddy teenage girl on a first date and had no idea what to do next. I giggled and then Brad giggled as well.

"Whatcha thinking?" I asked, while twiddling my thumbs.

"How much I want to kiss you right now," Brad said.

That was a surprise, and I felt a thrill shoot through my tense body.

He looked at me. "And what are you thinking?"

"I'm thinking we have about twenty-five minutes left. If you're gonna kiss me, you better start soon."

He leaned back on the couch and pulled me closer. I eagerly crawled over his reclining body and planted a kiss on his soft lips. I felt a rush of heat on my face. His hands caressed my back, and he closed his eyes. I ran my fingers through his hair and feasted on his soft lips. I didn't know what to expect, and I don't think Brad did either. We kissed softly at first; slow exploratory kisses and then little by little we kissed harder. I found my breath quicken as I darted my tongue into his mouth.

His hot breath told me he was enjoying himself as well. His hand grabbed my ass, and my pussy responded like a furnace through my jeans. I tugged at his shirt, and he obliged by yanking it off. I could barely pause before I was back kissing him again, my body pressed against his warm muscular chest.

We must have lost track of time because when I came up for air, sometime later, and glanced at the ornate wall clock, I had to do a double-take.

"Brad?"

"What?"

"We have like five minutes left. Damn, we never got to snuggle."

"You're kidding, right? We made out for twenty minutes already?"

I laughed and forced myself to climb off his lap. My hair was disheveled, and my blouse had come undone. I needed to orgasm, but that wasn't in the cards. My pussy ached and throbbed to be touched, but I wouldn't allow myself to take my jeans off. That was a line too far.

"We should get going," I said. We hadn't even turned on the television.

He made a sour face. I leaned into him and cradled his face in my hands and planted kisses on his lips until his pout became a reluctant smile.

"There will be other times," I whispered into his ear.

"Can I make one request, before we head back to work?"

I nodded. "Of course."

"Can I see your breasts?"

My eyes grew wide. I looked down at my half open blouse and thought there wasn't much Brad hadn't already seen today, so I agreed. Sitting upright I looked at his face. His large dreamy eyes eagerly waited to see what I would reveal. I slowly undid the rest of the buttons and slipped the blouse off my shoulders. I was sitting on his lap in only my jeans and my bra.

"The only man who has ever seen my bare breasts is my husband," I said quietly. *Did I want to expose my breasts to Brad? Did I want to cross this line? Yes, and yes again.*

"Your breasts will be perfect," Brad said. "Don't be nervous."

I blushed as I carefully reached behind my back and twisted the clasp on my bra. Then I brought the straps forward and down my arms before pausing. I covered my chest with my arms before pulling the bra free.

"You are nervous?" Brad asked as he caressed my arm.

I nodded and bit my lip.

"You don't have to do this if you don't want," Brad said. He picked up my bra and handed it back to me.

I shook my head and pushed his hand away. "No, it's not that, I want to show you. I'm just a little nervous, that's all.

I've ever only been with my husband. I mean, he's the only one who has ever seen them. God, I sound so weird."

"Take your time," Brad said softly.

I swallowed my courage, and lowered my arms. His eyes moved from my face to my breasts. I wanted to see his reaction. I don't have large breasts, and I was worried he wouldn't like them. My chest is a healthy c-cup, but I know many men like much bigger boobs. He stared for a moment with eyes wide. Then he leaned forward and braced my back in his arms and gently kissed each breast.

"They're beautiful," he whispered.

I couldn't help but smile as I wiggled my chest for him. "Really?"

"Can I touch them?"

"Of course."

He moved his arms from behind my back. I watched as he rubbed his hands together to warm them and then gently test the weight of each of my breasts. I smiled as he held them in his hands, like newborn babies. He gently squeezed, feeling their firmness and tweaking my nipples, before caressing his fingers around the sides. His tender manner contrasted sharply with the way my husband treated my breasts. I can't recall the last time I was touched so tenderly. I found Brad's gentle attention both alluring and erotic.

"Do you like them?" I asked, sounding more like a nervous school girl, and not a married woman.

"Your skin is so smooth and soft. There isn't a blemish anywhere. I can honestly say I haven't seen breasts like these in my entire life."

I laughed. "Now you're patronizing me. They aren't *that* great."

"They are yours, and I love them," Brad said. He leaned closer and rained kisses over each one. And I let him.

I glanced at the wall clock. We were out of time. *Just when things were getting interesting too.* I cursed my luck.

"I feel so bad," I confessed as I ran fingers through his hair. He looked at me questionably so I continued, "You must be so horny. I wish there was something I could do for you."

"You have," he said. "I'll be okay though, but I have to be honest with you, Julie. I can't remember ever being this hard. We need to get back to school or I might spend the afternoon sucking these gorgeous titties. Tell you what," Brad said, pausing for a moment. "How about we video chat tonight? Maybe you can help me take care of my erection?"

"You mean masturbate?"

He nodded sheepishly.

I liked his idea. "Deal. But for now we have to get going."

We dressed and tidied the seat cushions before scrambling out of the house. I was careful to lock the door. Back in the van, we raced to the school, the two of us laughing like naughty teenagers. After cranking the wheel into a vacant parking spot, Brad and I jumped out of the van and practically ran to our classes. I made it on time, winded, exhausted, but happier than I had been in years. I secretly hoped Brad wasn't late.

As I taught during the afternoon, I found it difficult once more to concentrate on my lesson plans. My pussy was soaking wet and dirty thoughts kept running through my mind. Dirty thoughts of Brad touching my breasts. Try as I might to focus on my job, I was struggling with sexual desire for the first time in my relationship with Brad.

When the last bell rang, I collected my things and rushed to the privacy of the teacher's washroom. Once inside, I locked the door to the stall and ripped down my jeans. I couldn't wait to orgasm and started to rub my clit furiously. My aching pussy responded immediately and within a minute I had a trembling orgasm. My fingers were slick with my wetness, but I didn't care. I rubbed out another while leaning against the inside of the stall. My legs trembled, and I tilted my head back and closed my eyes. Breathing heavily for a few minutes, I collected my thoughts. I felt dirty and extremely naughty. I had never masturbated in school before, but if I hadn't, I thought would have exploded.

Regaining my composure, I pulled my jeans up, unlocked the stall door, and washed my hands in the sink. A little cool water on my face was refreshing. I waited until my flushed cheeks returned to normal, tucked my hair back in place, adjusted my blouse and took a deep breath. I was ready to face the world again.

Later, when I got home with junior, I was pleasantly surprised to see that my husband had made dinner. I was shocked. While we ate, I found myself feeling aroused again but tried to put it out of my mind. I was going to help Brad masturbate later, during our secret video chat, and I thought I would probably flash him my breasts just to savor his expression once more. The idea that he would be looking at my bare breasts and jerking off, only made me feel more aroused and uncomfortable at the table. I barely finished my meal.

After we had cleared the dishes, I sat junior in front of the television and dragged my husband to the bedroom. He seemed perplexed until I wrapped my arms around him and started kissing him.

"Wow, what brought this on?"

I couldn't tell my husband that I was hot and bothered because I made out with a co-worker earlier was still horny. Instead, I came up with a suitable lie that Tim would believe.

"You made dinner, and it was so romantic I just had to jump you."

He grinned as I tore off his shirt. My husband was attractive at one time, and he still is if you turn off the lights. But, after four years of marriage, fatherhood had softened him. I loved him still, but I didn't like how quickly he had let himself go physically. Right now, though, I didn't care, and left the light on.

We tore each other's clothes off, and I pushed him onto the bed. His cock was rock hard, and I quickly straddled him. I needed something hard inside of me while I thought of Brad. When Tim reached for my breasts, I closed my eyes and imagined they were Brad's hands. I also imagined the cock inside of me was Brad's cock, and I quickly ground out a satisfying orgasm.

"Wow, you are wet!" Tim said.

"You make me so horny sometimes." It was a white lie, but no one was hurt. I kept riding my husband, but before my second orgasm could come, Tim grunted, grabbed my breasts roughly and erupted inside of me. Disappointed, I rode him as long as I could as he grew soft, but my orgasm faded away.

"Sorry," Tim said.

I removed his hands from my breasts and climbed off. "It's okay. I enjoyed myself."

By the time I had gone to the washroom and cleaned up, Tim was already downstairs playing his computer game. I didn't even get a snuggle or a thank you. Saddened, dressed and worked on my lesson plans while counting the hours until I could see Brad online.

By the time I bathed my son and tucked him into bed, I was more than ready to have another orgasm. I washed the dishes, tidied some toys and put my school bag by the front door, ready to go in the morning. With everything done, I eagerly flipped open my laptop and waited for Brad. *Hurry up!*

He wasn't online yet, but he had sent an email to my secret account that I hadn't noticed until I absently checked the inbox. I eagerly opened the message:

I won't be online until after eleven, sorry babe. But I do have a mission for you that I think will be fun. Open the following link, and see if you can name all the different bondage devices in the photo. Then I want you to click the second link and watch a video. I expect you to orgasm at least twice while watching it. Of course, you'll have to masturbate without your husband catching you. If you complete this assignment, email me. Then we can video chat. Don't disappoint me, Slut Slave. - Brad.

I read the email again. I was intrigued. I had never been called a slut slave before, and my knowledge of bondage was zero. I didn't even know what a slut slave was, but I think I had a pretty good idea. Brad's degrading language should have offended me, but it was obvious he was role playing. I felt like a dirty slut – his dirty slut – and I shivered with excitement. Could I be Brad's dirty secret whore, submitting to his every whim and desire without my husband ever knowing? The idea posed some challenges, but it also made my pussy grow warm. After the way he caressed me today, I was more than willing to try.

Clicking the link in the email brought me to a webpage depicting a bondage session. I looked up from my laptop and glanced towards the basement stairs. Through the floor, I could hear my husband's video game. He probably wouldn't be coming upstairs anytime soon, so I was safe. For now.

I glanced at my laptop and the photo again. There was a woman tied in a very stressful position, suspended with ropes. I could see red welts across her naked body from various whips. There was a bald man forcing his cock into the woman's open mouth. The woman had a ring harness keeping her jaws from closing, and it was obvious she had no choice but accept the man's cock. For some reason that made me horny. I spotted nipple clamps right away and also something inserted into the woman's anus with a fur-like tail. I had no idea what that was.

Opening my email, I started composing a reply to Brad's request and listed the nipple clamps and whips. I had to search the internet to find out the woman was wearing a spider gag. The object in her anus, I learned, was a butt plug. It was used to stretch a tight hole in preparation for anal sex. I cringed, imagining the pain and discomfort, but was fascinated at the same time. I had no idea people used such devices.

I examined the photo again, and added rope, a spreader bar, blindfold and a vibrator called a *magic wand* to my email. I didn't own any sex toys, but the idea of a vibrator suddenly made me eager to try some. After a double check that there were no other items in the picture I had to identify, I moved on to Brad's second challenge; masturbate to a video. I felt pleased with my little research project and hoped Brad would tell me that my answers were correct.

I turned the volume on my laptop to nearly mute, then took a deep breath, and clicked the video link. A website specializing in hardcore pornography popped up on my screen. Porn videos weren't my cup of tea. I knew my husband viewed such websites, but I had never visited one myself. Scores of naked women appeared in little boxes along the side of my screen promising videos of just about every imaginable sex act. I felt naughty as I waited for the video Brad had selected to start playing.

A young girl, probably eighteen or nineteen, with large bare breasts was facing the camera in the video. She wore Playboy bunny ears on the top of her blonde head. She had large blue eyes and a cute face. A large piece of duct tape covered her mouth preventing her from speaking. On her breasts were two clamps that bit into her nipples. A chain between the clamps had what looked like brass weights attached to it. It was a strange sight, and I waited to see what would happen.

I noticed the girl in the video had her arms either folded or tied behind her back, preventing her from easing the pain on her nipples. She started to bounce up and down, which of course caused the weighted chain to follow suit. Her heavy breasts flopped up and down, and I could see her wince each time her nipples stopped the falling momentum of the weights. I winced as well. I could imagine the discomfort the girl must be feeling, but she didn't slow or falter. Despite the pain, she was obeying whoever had instructed her movements. I guess whoever was filming this knew the men are watching would enjoy seeing a girl bouncing big weighted tits. I found that the tape across her mouth, muffling her whimpers, aroused me. I slipped my hand under my panties and started to finger my clit.

The more her tits bounced up and down, the more excited I felt. I didn't orgasm like Brad had commanded, and when the video finished I sighed. Not one to give up, I looked at the suggested videos under the one I just watched. There was a video of another large breasted girl using her tits to jerk off a man's cock. Intrigued, I clicked the video. I had no idea you could do that with your breasts.

This time, the video showed a slightly plump girl with thick breasts. I started rubbing my clit as I watched a man pour baby oil over a girl's chest while she rubbed it over her glistening globes. I imagined those were my breasts and rubbed my clit harder. The girl then took his cock and slipped it between her cleavage and pressed her breasts together. The man leaned back and seemed to be enjoying himself as she worked her big heavy breasts up and down his shaft. I could see his cock squeezed tightly between her young cleavage. Soon the man grunted, and his cock spurted cum all over her neck and chin much to the amusement of the girl. I gasped and felt my pussy quiver as I brought myself to orgasm. I had never watched another man besides my husband ever orgasm, and the newness of it, gave me a thrill. Could men really cum so much?

I pulled my wet fingers out of my panties and looked towards the basement stairs. There wasn't any sound from my husband's video game. I had a mild panic attack and quickly closed the program. My cheeks flushed. Moments later Tim strode up the stairs, and I caught sight of him heading into the kitchen. I opened my browser and pretended I was reading the news. A minute or two later, Tim walked into the living room and over to where I was sitting.

"Hey Honey, how's the gaming?" I asked, hoping he didn't notice my flush.

"Oh not bad, just got thirsty. Whatcha doing?"

"Oh, nothing. Just checked my email. I was bored and thought I'd see what's new in the world. You want to watch a movie or something? I need snuggles."

Tim downed the last of his beverage. "Sorry, got some friends logging on later. You know tonight is dungeon raiding night."

"Is it? Oh, I forgot. Well, have fun. I'll probably have a bath and head to bed soon. Want me to say goodnight so you can tuck me in?"

"I'd like to, but once we start the raid, I can't be stopping every five minutes to see what you need. You go on to bed without me. Sweet dreams."

I watched him walk away and disappear once again into the basement. I felt rejected, but also relieved. Tim hadn't caught me. His game was more important that spending time with his wife. Not even the hint that I'd be naked in the bath seemed to spark his interest in spending time with me. Moments later I heard his game through the floor once again. I wasn't going to be his servant forever.

I opened my browser and searched for the name of the video site I had just closed. Within thirty seconds I was back to it, and browsing erotic videos. Brad's email stated that I had to orgasm twice, so my mission wasn't complete yet. I just needed one more video to watch that would do the trick. Tonight's theme seemed to be breasts, so I typed that into the search engine. Hundreds of videos popped up, and I scrolled down until finding something intriguing. Most of the videos looked stupid, but then I stumbled upon a video of a woman on her knees with men all around her. She was cupping her breasts. I clicked play.

Sure enough, there was a college aged brunette kneeling on the floor, her face and hair done to perfection. I marveled that such an attractive woman would choose to do porn. Surely someone that beautiful didn't need to be a porn actress, I thought. She was playing with her large breasts while various men stuffed hard cocks into her mouth. She would suck each one for a while, alternating between each man in turn. I thought servicing six men with blowjobs, to keep them hard, was an impressive skill. I had tried performing oral on my husband once, and didn't like it. I know all men love blowjobs, but I never felt the urge to become practiced in the technique like the girl in the video obviously was. Maybe oral was something Brad could teach me? I tucked that thought away for later.

One of my secret fantasies was to be blindfolded and told to suck off men that I couldn't see, and men who I didn't know. I would have no choice but to suck any cock put in my mouth. I wouldn't be allowed to refuse, or to stop sucking until the man had an orgasm. I wouldn't have any say in whether the stranger cummed in my mouth, or all over my face, or across my breasts. Despite my inability to give blowjobs, the video reminded me of my fantasy, and I slipped my hand once more under my panties. My pussy was wet, and ready, as I fingered it.

One man in the video suddenly yanked his cock out of the girl's mouth and started stroking furiously. My interest perked. The girl cupped her breasts, offering them as a platter for him. I was fascinated and rubbed my clit harder. The man started spurting thick streams that splattered all over her chest. The girl was patient and waited with a smile on her face until he milked the last drops. She then went back to sucking a freshly offered cock without bothering to clean the mess. While she was sucking that man off, a third man stepped forward and ejaculated on the side of her face.

This parade of cocks continued, each man adding layers of glaze to her chest and face until they were all done. Once finished, the men walked away without so much as a thank you to the girl or a glance back. Eventually, she was the only one left in the scene. The camera panned a close-up of her cum splattered tits and face. She smiled, docile-like, and posed while casually scooping cum with her fingers and licking it. I wanted to be that girl.

I shuddered and gasped as my orgasm came. I rubbed my clit and squeezed my eyes shut while enjoying the waves of pleasure that radiated through my body.

I could get used to this.

With my task complete, I rested for a moment and caught my breath. Were there really women out there who did these sorts of things for the camera? I had to admit my knowledge of pornography was just a woeful as my knowledge of bondage. I felt like a neophyte amateur, and if it weren't for Brad, my horizons would never have grown larger. These videos opened a whole new world to me, and I was eager to explore.

I added a message at the bottom of the email telling Brad that his Slut Slave had accomplished her mission and cummed twice as commanded. I told him that his slave would be waiting patiently for Master to contact her later. I thought continuing the role playing was a nice touch. I knew Mr. Dork would smile and laugh. I sent the email and closed my laptop.

When eleven o'clock rolled around, my husband was deep into his online dungeon raid, and I was still waiting patiently by my laptop for Brad to message me. Finally, the message came:

Get in the bath, and bring your tablet.

I frowned. Brad could have told me that earlier and I would have had a bath drawn and ready. I replied that Slave would need a few minutes to prepare. Shutting down my laptop, I grabbed my tablet and hurried to the bathroom. After inserting the plug in the bottom of the tub, I started the water and added bubble bath. Using my tablet, I sent a message that the water was running.

Brad asked where my husband was. I told him Tim was still playing on the computer and that I could hear the noise of it through the floor. We won't be disturbed. While the tub was filling, I checked on my sleeping son and was pleased to see him out cold.

Returning to the bathroom, I closed and locked the door. Brad had sent a video chat request and a little pop-up was waiting for my acceptance. I clicked *accept* and then saw his face appear. He smiled, and I gave him a little wave.

"Can you hear me?" Brad said through his microphone headset.

I nodded and adjusted my volume down a little.

"Good," Brad said. "I want you to set the tablet on the edge of the sink so I can watch you undress."

I gasped in fake shock at the audacity of his request. I knew I'd be putting on a show for him, but I enjoyed role playing the startled innocent and watching the expression on his face. "Is that an order, Master?" I asked in a coy voice.

He nodded, and I watched him behind his desk, stand and remove his shorts and boxers before sitting back in his chair. He was getting ready to masturbate while watching me and I felt a naughty thrill travel up my spine.

I could see his eyes staring at me. Leaning the tablet behind the sink, I adjusted the angle until he gave me a thumbs up sign. I laughed. I couldn't believe I was going to give my co-worker an online strip tease in my own bathroom! Suddenly I wished I had dressed in sexy lingerie, but Brad hadn't given me any warning before we started. He would have to live with me stripping whatever I was wearing.

After double-checking that the bathroom door was locked, I started swaying my hips as if dancing to imaginary music. I undid my jeans, revealing my hot pink panties and slid them

42

down my hips a little. I then danced and swayed a slow circle until my back was to camera before pulling my shirt over my head. I hoped he could see the top of my butt and would be eager for more. Pulling the scrunchy out of my hair, I let my disheveled mane trail down my back. Giving my head a shake, I let my hair cascade haphazardly. Then, peering over my shoulder suggestively, I winked at Brad. His face was rapt with anticipation.

I turned to face him, and bent forward, yanking my jeans down my legs and giving him ample view of my breasts and cleavage swaying inside my bra. Brad was smiling. I unclasped my bra and flung it off my shoulders revealing my breasts to him for the second time. I was much less reticent the second time. Adopting a pouty expression, I played with my titties, cupping and squeezing them for Brad's viewing pleasure. My last article of clothing was my pink panties. I turned away once more and bent forward making sure he had a clear view of my rump. I swayed my hips and lowered my panties inch by inch until gravity took over and they slid down my slender legs. I was completely nude and aroused. Turning back towards the camera I smiled mischievously.

"How was that, Master?" I said as I leaned closer to the tablet and pressed my breasts together with my arms. I didn't want my husband to hear any voices in the bathroom, so I kept my voice low. I could still hear his game through the floor.

"Very nice, now get in the bathtub."

There was a nice mountain of soft bubbles forming on top of the bath water. I turned off the tap and with the tablet in hand, stepped into the water. It was warm, but not uncomfortable. I sank into the depths of luxurious bubbles.

"Are you enjoying yourself, Master?" I said quietly.

He nodded, and I could tell he was jerking off under the desk as he peered back. I wondered how long it would take Brad to bring himself to orgasm.

"What would you like Slave to do now?"

He grinned. "Set the tablet so I can watch you, and get your tits all soapy. I want to see you playing with them."

I nodded and leaned the tablet against the wall at the end of the tub. I had to be careful that the edge of the bathtub was dry. The last thing I wanted was to have my tablet to fall in the water and get ruined. Once satisfied my tablet was safe, I moved back from the camera and scooped warm water over my breasts. They soon became slippery and wet. A bottle of body wash caught my eye. I opened the bottle and squeezed thick strands of soap across my chest. Replacing the bottle, I then began to rub my breasts. A moan escaped my lips.

"Are you getting horny?" Brad asked.

"Yes, Master."

"Okay, you are permitted one orgasm."

"Thank you, Master."

It didn't take me long to orgasm once my warm fingers probed my clit and started rubbing. I briefly glanced at Brad, who was watching me intently, and then closed my eyes. I knew he could see my soapy breasts while he masturbated,

44

and that thought only made my orgasm more powerful. I gasped and rubbed harder. My face contorted as I brought myself over the edge. I was surprised at how powerful it was. Being watched while I masturbate was a definite turn-on.

"Very good, Slave. Now play with your tits some more, and tell me how much you want me to cum all over them," Brad commanded, his voice husky.

I looked at his face on the tablet. He was concentrating, and I didn't think he was going to last very much longer. If I could do anything to help him orgasm, then I was thrilled to do it. Grabbing my breasts, I rubbed and massaged and pressed them together while making soft moaning sounds, just like the girls in the videos I had watched.

"Please, Master. I want your cum, all over my tits," I begged softly.

He grunted, and I could tell he was jerking off even faster now.

"Please, Brad. I want your cum all over me. Please cum. I want to see it."

I guess the combination of my sultry begging and my slippery bare breasts pushed Brad over the edge at last. He grunted again, and I saw a flash of tissues as his other hand slipped below the desk. I pressed my breasts together and held them like two glistening melons as I watched the screen in fascination. His face contorted as he stared at my tits and started to cum. I felt a thrill of excitement. I had never made another man orgasm, other than my husband. I could see Brad look down sheepishly, and guessed he was cleaning up his mess.

"Did Slave please Master?" I asked in a quiet voice as I nibbled a finger suggestively, trying to look as innocent as possible.

Brad nodded and smiled back at me. "You did well, now finish your bath. I'll see you at work tomorrow."

"You're leaving me?" I asked in a slightly hurt tone.

"I have work to do. You did well. Master is pleased."

"Aright," I said with a pouty face. "I guess I'll go. Goodnight, Master."

"Goodnight, Slave," Brad replied. The video link went dead.

I turned off my tablet and wrapped it in a towel before setting it safely on the floor where it couldn't accidently get wet. Brad hadn't even thanked me, unless telling me I did well was his way of saying it. I felt used, but I loved it, and wanted more. I wanted to be used again. I wanted the power to make men orgasm. I wished I could have reached through the tablet and snuggled with him. I felt exhilarated that I had helped another man orgasm simply by playing with my bare breasts like a dirty whore. Leaning back into the bubbles, I closed my eyes and relaxed. My wandering hands found my clit again, and I slowly enjoyed another orgasm. This one, though, was for me alone.

That night I slept better than I had slept in years.

Discovering that Brad was into the whole bondage lifestyle had come as a bit of a shock to me. I was a complete neophyte when it came to anything bondage related. Until now, I had always thought bondage was for freaks and perverts, and I had never considered, or sampled, it's hidden pleasures. Now I wanted to experience it all.

Over the next few weeks, I asked Brad every question I could think of about bondage. He would always answer patiently, or give me a web page to read. I eagerly read everything he told me too, when my husband wasn't around of course. Soon Brad's answers turned into lessons, and he would assign me homework where I had to watch a video or research the rules of bondage. There was always something different he wanted to teach me and I devoured everything. I discovered safe words and hard limits. I also learned the relationship expectations between a Master and a Submissive. I found the videos and pictures very arousing and often masturbated secretly while looking at them.

One day Brad sent me a fictional story he had written about me. I was flattered and excited. When I read it that night, I was so wet and horny, that I gave myself three orgasms. Later, when he asked how I liked his story, I gushed and told him it was amazing. I told him he was a talented writer. He liked that and sent me more. Eventually, he asked if I wanted to try some bondage games. I asked him what sort of bondage games? Brad said just fun missions he would give me, and I would try to carry them out. If I failed any particular mission, I would, of course, be punished in a suitable way. I was a little apprehensive and worried my husband would grow suspicious, but I was willing to try.

It turned out Brad's bondage games were innocent things. One time, my mission was to find five household items that I could use for masturbation. He wanted to teach me that just about anything could be adapted for bondage play. Another time I had to write dirty words on my chest in the morning and wear them under my garments all day at school.

One of his most thrilling requests was for me to show up at school in a skirt and blouse while not wearing any panties. As a school teacher, this was extremely nerve wracking mission. Any one of my students could discover my secret. After I had built up the nerve to try (it took three days) I did finally complete his mission and taught students for an entire day without wearing any panties. My pussy was wet and soaked the entire time, which I think looking back, was Brad's plan all along.

We spent more time together at work and went out for coffee almost every lunch hour, where we would huddle like secret lovers in a coffee shop and talk endlessly. Every night we messaged back and forth, or he would email me a new story or delightfully new mission challenge.

While my husband and I became less intimate, I was finding emotional support and companionship with Brad to replace it. I felt like I could tell Brad anything, and in return, he opened new doors for me to explore. He showed me things I would never have known as a sheltered school teacher and lonely wife.

Over time we became physically closer too. At work, we would hug each other in the morning. At lunch, we held hands while sitting at the cafe. It wasn't long until we stole little kisses at every opportunity. Before Brad entered my life, my only kissing experience was once in the fourth grade, which doesn't count, and with my husband, which probably doesn't count either. It felt strange and exhilarating to secretly kiss another man. I think the thrill of being caught was part of its allure for me. As Brad and I spent more and more time together over the following months, I found myself falling in love with him.

Before I met Brad, if you had asked me was if it was possible to love two men at once, I would have declaratively said no. You can't love more than one man. Now, though, I wasn't sure. I loved my husband, but I also loved Brad.

One day Brad asked if I could buy headphones with a built in microphone like his so we could talk instead of always typing during our nightly sessions. I agreed and bought a headset the next day. We chatted and typed, and I lost myself in our friendship and felt my heart grow closer and closer to him. Every night when my husband went to the basement to play games, I would chat with Brad for hours. It seemed he understood me better than anyone. I had found my soul mate and developed an emotional bond with him to compensate for my husband's neglect. Like a wilted flower drinking water, I wanted more and more.

One night Brad asked me to read one of his stories to him. I asked him why do that? He knew how his stories ended. He said he didn't care about the stories, he just wanted to hear my voice reading something dirty while he masturbated. I laughed and asked him if he masturbated a lot while we chatted and was surprised when he said yes. I was stunned by his revelation. I thought the only time he had masturbated was when I gave him the strip tease in the bathtub.

He revealed he'd jerked off practically every night while we chatted, or while he was thinking dirty things about me. I was flattered and a little surprised. I confessed I had masturbated to his stories, but never while we chatted. Brad told me he would love to hear me masturbate with the headphones on so he could hear it. My face flushed at the idea that just my voice reading dirty stories could make him orgasm. I agreed to do it for him if he read one of his stories for me also.

The first time I listened to Brad's voice in the dark, reading an erotic tale, I had the most powerful orgasm of my life. Soon I was masturbating practically every night to his voice, or while looking at dirty pictures he sent me. It seemed our relationship was growing deeper and deeper, and I felt more and more comfortable doing physical things with him.

Feeling bold one night in January, I suggested to Brad, that if he was jerking off while thinking about me, then perhaps I should send him some topless pictures to help him. He liked the idea.

My first few selfie attempts were ridiculous and out of focus, but in time, and with Brad's help, I was able to pose better and sent him pictures whenever he wanted. I even wen so far as to categorize my lingerie by laying them all on my bed and sending him photos. Using my makeshift photo catalogue, he would request different outfits, mixing and matching what appealed to him. I would then dress and pose for him. Sometimes he would request I write things on my body and send him a picture. I found it difficult to write upside down on my breasts, but eventually I got the hang of it.

One day in March I told Brad that I loved role-playing his slut-slave, but I wanted to take it a step further. He asked me what I meant. I said I would love to be a slut-slave in real life. I wanted to enter into a formal Dominant/Submissive relationship. Brad seemed surprised but happy. He said he would gladly be my Dom if I would be his Submissive, so long as my husband never found out.

And that's how things progressed from searching for sandwiches at the start of the school year, to me formally entering into a sexual contract to be Brad's submissive in the spring. I wanted to be obedient and follow his every order like a willing school girl. I willingly gave control of every aspect of my sexuality to Brad, in exchange for his mentoring and promise to always protect me.

My sexual arousal spiked and I felt like a brand new world had just opened up for me. Brad introduced me to vibrators and the joys of thick rubber dildos, even going so far as to picking the ones online that I should buy. I bought what he suggested and loved it. Wanting to please him, I took the initiative and invited Brad to the video stream with me while I tried out my new sex toys. I loved to masturbate for him. Brad often sent me email photos of how hard he had cummed. I loved it. During my entire sexual awakening with Brad, my husband never once became suspicious. I felt like I was leading a double life. In a way, I guess I was. Tim had his computer games, but Brad had a submissive sex slave. I didn't need to think very hard to know who had the better deal. I was in heaven.

Over the course of our secret affair, we've had maybe two dozen occasions where we were alone together with privacy outside of our teaching jobs. I was more than eager to keep adding to that number, so long as Brad continued to be my emotional rock. Being married and having a child, though, does make the opportunities of alone time with another man somewhat difficult at times. So when a chance comes, I don't like wasting a moment. After all, a submissive slave must always look for opportunities to please her master.

I was eager and willing to take our relationship to the next level and expressed my desires to Brad. So far we had been lucky; my husband hadn't discovered my infidelity, nor noticed the array of lingerie and sex toys that was accumulating in my dresser drawers.

"Are you ready to take our relationship to the next level?" Brad asked me early one morning in June. We were sitting in the English Office getting exams ready for the end of the school year. I did want to experience more in our relationship, and he knew it. I felt so liberated and free with Brad, and I wanted to taste everything life had to offer with him.

"Yes, Master," I replied.

"I think there is one thing you will need to learn if you are going to become a truly dedicated submissive under my control."

I put my exam papers on the desk and gave Brad my full attention.

"Blowjobs," Brad said.

My eyebrows rose in surprise. "Really now? I'm guessing you want me to start sucking you off every lunch hour?"

Brad blinked. "That's a brilliant idea. I hadn't even thought of that. Yes!"

I rolled my eyes. "I've only tried it once, and I hated it. I'm afraid you will be sorely disappointed in my lack of skills."

Brad only smiled and nodded his head. "We will start today then."

"Oh, will we?" I said in defiant jest. "You think you can just order me to suck your cock whenever you want?"

Brad nodded. "You know the storage garage where they keep the winter snow clearing equipment?"

I felt a thrill course through my body. Brad always had a plan. Did he really want me to suck his cock? Of course he did. All men love blowjobs. I should have thought of this sooner and at least practiced on a sex toy. The prospect of performing oral, both frightened and excited me at the same time.

"I know they store the winter stuff in there somewhere," I said after a moment. "But I've never been in there, no."

"Like the time you had a key to your friend's house back in the fall, I have a key to the winter storage garage," Brad said triumphantly.

"I thought only custodians had access. How did you get a key?"

"I volunteered to do setup the safety cones last winter for the school buses and the office gave me a key. I guess no one ever asked for it back."

I felt my cheeks flush at the prospect of finding a secret place and having some fun with Brad. What if I was terrible at blowjobs? Who was I kidding? I knew I was terrible at it. I didn't want to displease him. My mind reasoned that I should stall for time and spend the next few nights practicing on a sex toy. I could probably find a website that explained how to perform oral sex on a man too.

"I don't know," I said reluctantly. "It seems risky. What if someone finds us?"

Brad laughed. "It's June. No one will be going in there until it's time to do maintenance on the snow blowers and stuff. Heck, I bet no one has even been in there since that last snowfall in March."

"I'm just nervous."

"That's why you need to trust your Dom. I won't risk us getting caught. At lunch, we'll sneak in. I know a spot with chairs and a couch where the custodians used to sit and drink hot chocolate when they thought no one was looking."

"Brad, I don't know how...you know," I paused in exasperation.

"What is it? What's wrong?"

"Brad, I don't know how to suck a cock," I blurted. There, I said it.

My admission made Brad laugh, and I felt my cheeks flush.

"That's why I'm going to teach you. Practical teaching every day, plus extra homework for you at home. I like the idea of you sucking on my cock. You will do this for Master," Brad said.

I bit my lip.

Brad wasn't impressed with my silence. "What do you say?"

"Yes, Master," I replied. I could feel a tingle in my pussy. The very idea that he was commanding me to suck him off, and that I had no choice made me feel like the dirty whore in my fantasies. Of course, if I truly wanted to refuse, then Brad would relent. One of the most important things I had learned over the past months about the Dominant and Submissive relationship, is that the submissive has all the power. Giving up her power willingly, the submissive woman allows the dominant male to take control. But the key, I learned, was that the dominant has no power unless the submissive grants it.

"Good," Brad said. "I'll meet you at the storage room at noon. I'm going to check that my key still works. How do you feel about swallowing cum?"

I did a double-take. "Pardon?"

"Have you ever considered swallowing my cum?"

I shook my head. "To be honest, I have never even thought of it."

"Would you be willing to try?"

The thought of swallowing his ejaculate made my stomach churn. I had no idea what semen tasted like, and I was afraid I would hate it. On-the-other-hand, if I was going to take this journey down the dark path, then I had to be willing to experiment with new things. But could I swallow cum? I guessed I could try it at least once if it really meant a lot to Brad for me to do it.

"If Master wishes, Slave will obey," I said meekly.

"Great. I can see the worry on your face. We'll start slow, trust me, I won't make you do anything you aren't comfortable with, and I won't push you. Master is happy. You're turning into quite the obedient little slut-slave."

I smiled at his compliment. "Thank you, Master."

"See you at lunch," Brad said as he left me alone in the English Office.

I stared at the empty doorway for a moment wondering what I was getting into. I had sucked my husband's cock once and it scared me. Tim tried to ram it down my throat and I remember panicking. I trusted Brad, though. He wouldn't hurt me, or make me feel uncomfortable. Though I was getting aroused by the idea of making Brad cum with my mouth, I was nervous about swallowing and even more nervous of being discovered. If we were caught, it would mean the end of our teaching careers.

Could I perform oral sex on school property? I had already masturbated maybe a dozen times in the privacy of the teacher's washroom without Brad knowing—or anyone else for that matter. I was turning into a dirty slut, but not a dirty slut for anyone, just Brad. I smiled.

Once again I struggled to plow through my morning classes. My thoughts kept returning to my conversation in the English Office. I knew I should be offended that another man ordered me to suck his cock. In today's era of political correctness, men just didn't speak to women that way. Perhaps it was because I was so used to PC, that it turned me on when a man so flagrantly crossed the line. It was taboo. I knew I needed some space and time alone to ponder the source of my dirty excitement. I was certain there was some psychological component to the entire dominant and submissive relationship. Perhaps it was power, or the lack thereof. I didn't know, and I couldn't fully explore these thoughts in the midst of teaching my English class, so I pushed them aside.

I felt a mild panic when the lunch bell rang. I glanced at the clock. My palms felt sweaty. I was about to march down to the storage garage and put a man's cock in my mouth for only the second time in my life. I could refuse, of course, but that would ruin the entire role playing power dynamic. Who was I kidding? There was no role playing power dynamic. I was just plain nervous about giving Brad a blowjob.

Gathering my lesson plans, and shutting off the classroom lights, I casually made my way towards our secret rendezvous. Some students were milling around their lockers while others were rushing this way and that. I began to wonder how I was supposed to slip into the storage garage unobserved. Wouldn't any student who spots a male and female teacher sneaking into an off limits area of the school not raise suspicions? Gossip would spread. Students would talk. Teachers would overhear and the Principle would get involved. We would be discovered. My heart was pounding in my chest and I was certain I had *sexual deviant* written across my forehead for everyone to see. I began to consider that this might not be a good idea after all.

As I approached the door to the storage garage, it suddenly opened. I jumped, startled because of my nerves. Brad stepped into the hallway and glanced at me.

"Hello, Mrs. Snow. I was just about to find someone to help me move some heavy boxes." Some nearby students glanced up but then went back to their conversations and smartphones. "If it wouldn't be a bother, could you assist me for a moment?"

I recovered from the shock and suppressed a smile. Of course, Brad would have thought of a plan. I nodded and in a loud enough voice to be heard by nearby students, I agreed.

"But only for a little," I admonished. "I have important meetings to attend before lunch is over."

"It won't take but a moment, Mrs. Snow," Brad said holding the door for me.

I winked at him as I stepped into the garage and then turned and watched him close the heavy door behind us and heard the unmistakable clanking sound of the lock. We were alone.

"Is it secured?" I asked quietly.

Brad nodded. "This way, follow me."

I trailed behind him as he wove his way around large tractors and snow throwing equipment, then around some stacked wooden crates that revealed tattered and worn couches and chairs. A stained coffee table, that had seen better days, rested in the middle of the makeshift lounge.

"So this is where the custodians hide?" I said in amazement.

"Only in the winter. They have other hiding spots we probably don't even know about all over the school. We don't have much time. Are you ready?"

"I'm scared, but I'm ready."

"Good, kneel on the floor here," Brad instructed as he began to undo his cargo pants and pull them open.

Just like that? No talking. No caressing. Just kneel on the shag carpet and start sucking? I felt like a dirty whore as I watched the man I love pulling out his cock. I wanted desperately to please him, so I ignored my fears of inadequacy and carefully knelt on the pale green shag carpet.

"What do I do?" I asked as I peered at his growing cock which he was stroking it in anticipation. "Remember, I've only done this once."

"Not a problem. Just open your mouth."

I did what he said and opened my mouth. My lips were dry, and I licked them nervously as I peered up at Brad's downward face. He appeared to be enjoying our session already. When I felt his cock touch my lips, my eyes darted down. The head of his shaft was thicker than I expected and I opened my mouth wider. My nostrils flared as my breathing quickened. He moved his cock forward, and I felt the weight of it slide across my tongue. I didn't know what to do so I remained still, my mouth open and my eyes blinking nervously.

Now, what?

Brad seemed to read my thoughts. "Close your lips around my cock. That's it, good girl. Now move your tongue around. Get used to the taste."

I obeyed and slid my tongue back and forth under the head of his cock. Not sure if I was doing it right, I peered up, my blue eyes blinking like an innocent school girl. His smile told me I had started well.

"Now, move your head forward and let my cock slide as far as it will go into your mouth," Brad instructed. "I want to see how much you can take."

I nodded and carefully moved my head forward until the thick head hit the back of my mouth and then I gagged and coughed. Brad created a ring around his cock with his hand before quickly withdrawing.

"Not bad," Brad said. He examined the portion of his cock that was in my mouth. "I'd say that was about four inches."

My urge to throw up subsided but my eyes started to water.

"Is that good?" I asked as I wiped my eyes clear.

"For a beginner, you did very well. Almost down your throat on your first try? You might be a natural at this, Julie," Brad said.

"Really?" I felt oddly euphoric.

He nodded. "Now let's try again. This time, I will stand still, and you move your head back and forth. It's important to use your tongue on the underside of a man's cock. That's where most of his pleasure comes from."

"Oh," I said. "I didn't know that."

I opened my mouth and wiggled forward on my knees until I could catch the tip of his cock with my mouth. He obliged me by tilting his erection downward. I slipped him into my mouth as far as I could and then started flicking my tongue.

"Don't forget back and forth with your head."

I had forgotten that part already. I started moving back and forth while flicking my tongue. I didn't know there were so many steps to remember when giving a blowjob. He was thick and I barely got half his cock into my mouth. I knew from watching porn that the professional girls could take the entire shaft of a man down their throats, but my gag reflex was so strong I feared that would never be a skill I could call my own.

"Ouch! Teeth, teeth!" Brad cried.

Brad yanked his cock from my mouth, and I looked up at his wincing face.

"You can't bite or scrape it with your teeth. That is the most important rule. Ouch, that hurt."

"I'm sorry," I said. I hadn't thought how much something like teeth would hurt. I hadn't thought about my teeth at all. If it was such an important rule, why hadn't Brad mentioned it first?

"Very sensitive. Okay, let's continue. This time, do the same as you were doing but don't let your teeth touch my cock. It's crucial if you want to make a man cum with your mouth to develop a rhythm. Try to find something that works for you and keep doing it. Pausing or slowing ruins the buildup of sensations. Are you ready to try again?"

I nodded and opened my mouth again. Brad slipped his cock into my mouth once more, and I closed my lips around the girth. I was very conscious of my teeth, this time, and started to move my tongue around the underside of his cock.

"Much better. Focus on the cock. It's all that matters to you."

I concentrated on keeping a rhythm and not scraping my teeth. I was so nervous that I was doing it wrong that I kept peering up at Brad's face for validation. He seemed to enjoy my wide blinking eyes and smiled down at me.

"Now, because you are new, there is quite a lot of my cock not being stimulated. When you see that much cock not in your mouth, you need to grip the exposed portion with your hand, and stroke in time with your head movements. It's crucial to always stimulate the entire cock, never just the tip."

I understood and reached up with my hand and wrapped it around his shaft. I wasn't sure if Brad had a huge cock or not, but it was thicker and longer than Tim's was. Part of me was curious what a big delicious cock like Brad's would feel like buried in my pussy.

"Very good. Now while you stroke with your hand in unison with your head movements, I want you to start twisting your wrist. Think of my cock as a motorcycle throttle. With each stroke, you want to rev that throttle up and down."

I suppressed a giggle and felt my teeth gently graze his shaft. Brad winced, and I looked up with an apologetic furrow of my brow. He cursed quietly. I had to be careful to keep my mouth wide. My jaw ached a little because I wasn't use to holding my mouth open for so long.

I moved my wrist as Brad instructed while I stroked his cock. There was a lot of steps involved in giving a proper blowjob. I had to be careful not to bite. I had to keep a steady rhythm. I had to move my head back and forth in unison with my hand strokes and I also had to twist my wrist back and forth. There were so many parts to a blowjob that could go wrong.

"Very good. Grip a little harder. Yes, that's it. Now with your free hand, I want you to cup my balls. Cup them with your other hand, and massage them gently."

Another step? I cupped his balls and they felt strange. I had never touched a man's balls before. Now I had to keep rhythm, stroke, and twist, grip harder, watch my teeth and play with his balls? How did anyone ever become good at this?

"Very good. Now increase your pace. Yes, a little more. Good, that's perfect. Maintain that until I cum," Brad said as he crossed his hands behind his back.

Until he cums? I blinked in fear. Was he going to cum in my mouth? I did as I was told, gripping harder and moving quicker as I thought about what he had just said. Did I want him to cum in my mouth? I've never tasted cum. It had never crossed my mind, but if there were one man in the world who I would allow to try such a thing, it would be Brad.

A few minutes later I was growing tired. He placed a hand on my head, guiding me as I worked. A soft moan escaped his lips, and I felt him buck his hips ever so slightly each time I moved my head forward. He was already poking my gag reflex. My eyes watered, and I sucked in as much air as I could through my nose. How much longer would this take? My jaw was aching, and I was starting to really tire.

"Do you want me to cum in your mouth, slut slave?"

I hesitated in responding, and Brad frowned. I quickly nodded my approval, feeling uncertain, as I continued to suck and stroke.

"Here it comes," Brad said and yanked his cock from my grasp. "Open your mouth and tilt your head back. Perfect just like that, now hold still."

I waited; mouth open and head tilted back, and watched him jerk off. He was much more rough with his cock than I was. My heart was thumping in my chest. I was about to get my first facial and I had no idea what to expect. Would I enjoy it like the girls in those porn videos? In a moment I was about to find out.

Grabbing the top of my head in a vice-like grip, Brad leaned closer, the head of his cock aimed at my open mouth. I stuck out my tongue like the women do in the porn videos. There was nothing to do but wait.

Sucking in his breath, Brad stopped jerking off for a moment, tensed all his muscles and then resumed his stroking. A second later a powerful thick stream of cum shot into my mouth hitting the back of my throat. I wasn't expecting such force and flinched my face, squeezing my eyes shut. Another two squirts hit the same spot. I tried to swallow but gagged instead and coughed. I turned my head away, which threw off Brad's aim, and another glob snaked across my cheek and into my ear. I moved my head back, still coughing and got another wad right up my nose followed by another globule in my eye. I began to panic. There was too much cum! I wretched and spit the cum out of my mouth and waved my arms frantically.

Brad ignored me and continued to spurt, this time hitting my hair and forehead.

I felt his rough hand grab my hair and yank my face up. It hurt, and I peered upwards through a watery eye. He still hadn't stopped jerking off and was holding my face under his cock and milking the last droplets onto my skin. When the last of his cum had been drained from his cock, Brad released my hair.

"Clean it," Brad ordered. I could tell by his tone that he was annoyed.

What did he mean clean it? I had no tissues or napkins. Was I supposed to get some? When I didn't move, he grew even more annoyed.

"Open your mouth and clean my cock."

Oh. I didn't know that was part of the process. I obeyed, hoping my willingness to follow instructions might take the edge off Brad's disappointment. I sucked and slurped his shaft and could already feel it starting to soften. The tip of his cock oozed cum, and I licked it clean with my tongue. I wasn't sure how long I was supposed to clean, so I kept sucking. He pulled it out when he had enough and tucked his cock away in his boxers. I watched as he pulled up his pants and zipped his fly.

"How did I do?" I asked. My face and lips were plastered with sticky spunk. Was I supposed to remain kneeling with his cum all over my face and hair? I wasn't sure.

"It was amateur at best. You need a lot of practice."

"You didn't like it?" I asked through cum stained lips. I felt crestfallen.

"Not really. You got lazy with your teeth and scraped me a few times. Then you insulted me by gagging and spitting my cum all over the carpet. You didn't hold still either. From now on, proper oral skills are something you're going to focus on. I can't have a slut-slave who doesn't even know how to give a proper blowjob."

I hung my head in shame and carefully scooped cold cum out of my one eye. I could feel more of it cooling on my face, and I didn't even want to know how much he got in my hair. I had to teach a class soon. I couldn't walk in on students with cum in my hair!

"I told you I wasn't good at it, Brad. I'm sorry you didn't like it. Please, let me practice and I promise to do better. It was just so much to learn right away."

"I'll think about it," Brad said as he plopped himself on one of the chairs.

"Do you have any tissue?"

"What for?"

I thought it was obvious. "My face. I have to clean this off before I teach."

My statement seemed to make Brad upset.

"What's wrong?" I asked, feeling truly bewildered.

"If this was a normal relationship, then yes using a tissue would be appropriate. But what kind of relationship do we have, Julie?"

"A Master and Slave relationship?" I answered carefully.

"That's right. What do you think should happen if a slave spills her master's cum on the floor or gets it on her face when it was supposed to go in her mouth?"

I swallowed my nerves. What was he suggesting? "Slave licks it up?"

"Who are you addressing right now?"

"Slave licks it up, Master?"

"Much better. You must always show proper respect. While we're on this subject, you also failed to thank me for the privilege of servicing my cock."

"I did? I mean I am supposed to thank you?"

Brad shook his head in dismay. "I thought you were learning things from those websites I had you visit. Yes, you always thank a man for using you, and you never spill his cum."

I didn't know what to say. I thought he would have been more grateful. I had never seen Brad so upset before. He leaned forward in his chair and reached for a spoon sitting in one of the old coffee cups on the table. He handed me the spoon, and I took it nervously. What was this for, I wondered and how long had that spoon been sitting there?

"Scoop the cum off your face and eat it. Then get your face into that carpet and slurp that mess up too," Brad said in a serious voice.

I felt degraded, but I nodded. Glancing at the spoon didn't make me feel any better. The surface of the spoon was tarnished with old dried coffee. I brought the edge against my skin and carefully scraped Brad's cum off my skin. I glanced at what I had collected and cringed inwardly. I had to eat it now? Like sour medicine, I put the spoon in my mouth and swallowed without tasting. I could feel it slide down my throat, and I resisted the urge to vomit. I felt degraded.

Brad was smiling. I continued to scoop and scrape my face and cheek until I could find no more, and then swallowed it all. He pointed towards the carpet, and I sighed with resignation. Eating spilled semen off a dirty carpet was beyond humiliating. I lowered myself on all fours until my face was staring at the thick collection of sperm resting within the fibers of the shag carpet. I glanced at Brad but his face was stern, and he pointed to the spot on the carpet once more. His demeanor said he expected obedience.

I shuddered and lowered my lips to the congealed mess and slurped it in quick short bursts. I could only get the surface material because I didn't want to get surface fibers and lint in my mouth.

"I still see cum on that carpet. Get your face into it and suck each strand of carpet until it's clean."

I wanted to cry, but I obeyed. Brad's happiness was the most important thing in the world to me. I pressed my lips into the carpet and felt my stomach revolt. I wretched but fought it and licked and sucked as best I could. When I sat up, strands of hair and specs of carpet clung to my lips and face. I had never felt so dirty and used in my life and yet my pussy throbbed with desire.

"Much better, Slave. Now you may use that sink in the corner and make yourself presentable, but not until you thank me," Brad said.

"Thank you, Master," I said through cum soaked lips. My cheeks burned with humiliation. There was a hair on my tongue.

"Very good, now clean up."

"Yes, Master." I staggered to my feet and quickly rushed towards the sink. My stomach was about three seconds from emptying itself, and it took all my willpower to keep everything down. I flicked the tap on, not even caring how old the water in the pipes had been and cupped my hands under the flow. I flushed my mouth out first, spitting everything into the sink. Next, I wiped my lips and face clean with wet hands. Lastly, I gripped the sides of the sink and bent my face close to the water stream and drank huge quantities.

A dusty mirror on the wall above the sink offered no reflection. I grabbed a paper towel and ran it under the water then cleaned the mirror until I could see myself. Just as I feared, there was a thick strand of Brad's cum tangled in my hair. I took another paper towel, soaked it, and then tried my best to clean it.

While I was scrubbing, Brad sauntered over and watched me. I glanced at him in frustration and went back to cleaning my hair.

"If anyone sees this, I'm in a ton of trouble," I said.

"I understand."

"Do you? This stuff is like glue. It doesn't come out!"

"With practice, you will do better. Hurry up, slut. I have things to do."

I bit my tongue and scrubbed as best I could. My hair was wet now, and I took handfuls of paper towel and tried to dry it.

"Let me inspect it," Brad offered.

I felt some relief as he tilted my head towards the light and looked.

"I think you're good. I'm still annoyed that you have next to no ability to pleasure a man properly. I guess you weren't kidding when you said you were new at this."

"I told you I had no idea what to do! Real life isn't like those videos."

"Well, I have a plan to remedy the situation. Every night you will spend at least fifteen minutes sucking one of your rubber dildo toys. I want you to practice relaxing your throat and your gag reflex."

I remained silent, not trusting myself to speak civilly.

"Not every day, but at least three times a week during our lunch, we will find a place for you to show me your progress. I expect you to swallow."

I tossed a scrunched up paper towel ball into the trash can. "You want me to suck your cock three times a week now?"

Brad stepped closer, and for a moment I thought he was going to hit me, but instead he wrapped his arms around my shoulders and drew me in.

"This is important to me. I love you, and I love what we have together."

"I love you too," I whispered. I felt comforted by Brad's strong arms around me. Perhaps I was overreacting.

"Don't you want me to be happy?" Brad asked quietly.

I nodded and sniffled. I felt a tear roll down my cheek.

"Then do this for me, Julie. I want you to be good at sucking me off. I love blowjobs, so this is very important for me. Promise you'll try?"

"I promise, Master."

Brad stroked my hair as I rested my head on his chest. I did want him to be happy. I feared that he would end what we had together if I angered him. Part of me had also feared that I would disappoint him, and I was right. I had no idea how to give a proper blowjob and should never have tried.

"I can't believe I'm saying this, but I want you to start offering blowjobs to your husband too."

"What?" I pulled back and looked into his eyes. "You can't be serious."

"I am. I want you to get all the practice you can. Get under Tim's desk at home and tell him you want to suck him off while he looks at porn. Tell him you would rather give him a blowjob than have sex. Offer it every day. Beg for it."

"Every day?"

"Yes. I have a few friends I want you to suck off, in time."

I gasped. "Strangers?"

"Remember how many times you said your fantasy was to be used by men you didn't know?"

I nodded. Trapped by my own words.

"Well consider this a graduation exam. Who owns your mouth?"

"You do, Master," I replied meekly.

"And who owns your body?"

"You, Master."

"Then is it not my right to offer the services of my slut slave to others?"

I had nothing to say.

I waited by the front window and watched for Brad's car. After a while, I glanced at the wall clock and realized it had only been twenty minutes since I had texted him. Maybe I was a little too eager. My husband had taken our son to the amusement park so mommy could have a day to herself. That meant I was home all by my lonesome. Considering that I was Brad's secret slut-slave, I quickly informed Master that I was available for use. It wasn't easy getting my husband and my little monkey out of the house, so when it happened, I had to act fast. I wanted to devote every free moment I had to my Master. While I waited, I sent another text to Brad, asking that if there was time, did he want me to dress up for him?

He replied: *black corset, no panties, no bra, black teddy. Hair in a ponytail and a touch of that expensive perfume your husband bought you.*

I happily replied that Slave would obey. I needed to temper my excitement and understand that Master will arrive when he wants, not when I want. My duty was to obey his commands and wait on him to make my decisions for me.

Once dressed and ready, I glance again at the wall clock. Thirty minutes. Like a lonely school girl, I continued to wait by the front window watching for Brad's car. I couldn't wait to be alone with him. My pussy was already soaked, and I desperately wanted an orgasm, if Brad would permit me.

I finally spotted the red car rounding the corner. Clapping my hands in glee, I rushed to the door and waited impatiently. Just as Brad reached the first step, I opened the door and peeked around the frame. I had to be careful to hide my outfit, though, from anyone on the street. He looked up in surprise, but I ducked out of sight before he could speak. As Brad stepped into the house, I stood obediently with my arms at my side. He looked me up and down. I know my eyes were supposed to be lowered to the ground, but I had to steal a peek at him. His smile made the time and effort I spent getting dolled up, worth it.

"Slut-Slave is happy to see, Master," I said softly.

He took off his sunglasses, and tossed them on the kitchen table, while I took a moment to close and lock the front door. I couldn't contain my grin as I rushed into his arms as he turned. It felt great to hug Brad without my husband around – without anyone around actually. Just the two of us. It had been far too long.

Brad's hands trailed up and down my back before cupping my ass cheeks. I loved when he took liberties with my body and grabbed my ass or slipped a hand down my blouse without asking. My body was his to enjoy, and I was okay with it. I looked into his eyes and kissed him on the lips. I finally felt safe and secure in the arms of the man I had grown to love. Every second I could spend with him was precious to me, and I could barely contain my excitement.

"How long does Tim have the kid?" Brad asked as I snuggled into his shoulder. His hands lazily continued to squeeze my ass cheeks.

"Husband took him to the amusement park for the day. After he wants to try a new pizza place for dinner, so I'm not expecting him for hours."

"So we can do anything we want?" Brad asked.

His breath caught in his throat as I dropped to my knees and undid his shorts with vigor. I gave him a mischievous grin when he looked down at what I was doing. Then I yanked his shorts and boxers down. His semi-hard cock popped up, and I gazed at it lovingly. I had been secretly practicing my deep throat skills on a rubber dildo and was eager to show Master what I had learned. Memories of my failure in the storage garage still brought me shame, and I was determined to make up for my failings.

I had been dreaming of his cock more and more lately and was aching to feel it inside of me. The only problem was we couldn't have sex, no matter how much I craved it because I could become pregnant. Penetration was just out of the question. Despite my urges, I was fine not having sex with Brad, but the constant temptation was getting harder and harder to resist. At least for me. Luckily, there were other ways a woman could please her lover – especially if she practices – besides sex.

I gripped his cock and opened my mouth. Brad held very still, his eyes peering down at me in wonder as I slipped him between my warm lips. All that mattered now was keeping

Brad's cock happy. Brad understood me more than any man, and he gave me a zest that my husband never did. He was thoughtful and caring, and I was desperate to do anything that kept our relationship going. If that meant learning to give better blowjobs, then I was more than willing.

"Wow, I wasn't expecting this!" Brad said.

Taking his cock out of my mouth, I stroked it tenderly and looked into his eyes. "I want you to relax, Master. Relax and cum in Slave's mouth so that she can taste it. I want to swallow it all."

"Are you ready to take that next step?" Brad asked, his face concerned. Although we had talked before about that day in the storage garage, and how I had gagged and choked and spit his semen out, he had the impression I wasn't willing to try again. He was wrong. If some eighteen-year-old strumpet in a porn video could deep throat and swallow spunk for another porn actor, then I could do the same, and better, for the man I loved.

I've sucked him off six or seven times since that day, each time working on my technique and rhythm. But each time, right before he was about to cum in my willing mouth, he pulled out and used a tissue instead. I loved that he respected me enough to do something like that instead of painting my face or filling my mouth, but I wanted in my mouth. I needed to show him I could do it.

The last time I gave Brad a blow job, I begged him to give me a facial. He was surprised by my request and more than a little hesitant. Once he was satisfied that I really meant it, he finished my blowjob by jerking off furiously and splattering hot semen all over my face and hair. I didn't flinch or turn away, but held my face perfectly still, allowing him to spurt wherever he wished. And I loved it. Now I wanted it in my mouth, and I wanted to swallow it all.

I giggled. "I want you to fill my mouth with cum, Sir."

Brad smiled at me. "Master is pleased with his slut-slave."

I quickly get back to work. Brad's cock wasn't thick like my husband's, but it was longer and smoother. I liked the feel of it in my hand, and I loved the taste of it in my mouth. A video I watched the other day reminded me of the importance of maintaining a rhythm. I already knew not to touch or graze his cock with my teeth and all those other important steps to performing successful oral. The jewel in the crown was to develop more stamina, and my blowjob skills would rival any porn starlet. I was grateful that Brad had instructed me to suck my husband off as much as possible, even though at first I was reluctant. Blowjobs didn't solve my marital woes, but it did make Tim a much happier husband, and I got a lot of much-needed practice on my unsuspecting guinea pig.

While stroking and sucking, I also gently caressed Brad's balls. A smart slut-slave learns to better her skills so she can please her Master. By the look on his face, Brad was enjoying his treat.

It didn't take long before Brad groaned, and I felt his cock twitch in my hand. Keeping a steady unmerciful rhythm was the key to making a man cum fast. I quickly sealed my lips and gave him firm, steady jerks with my hand. Moments later

78

he spurted in my mouth. The force of it always catches me off guard, and I always flinch. I'm not sure I'll ever not flinch. I could barely contain my excitement as thick hot streams of his semen filled my mouth. I felt my cheeks filling, and felt mild alarm, but I didn't stop stroking. Brad usually never shot this much spunk. It was nearly too much, and some escaped the corners of my mouth and trickled down my chin. I hoped he wasn't disappointed in my performance. Brad gets very irate whenever I spill his cum. Apparently, a slave girl is expected to treat a man's ejaculate with reverence and respect. Letting cum fall to the ground or drip out of your mouth was an insult.

"Don't swallow it!" Brad said as I milked the last drops into my mouth, my cheeks are puffed.

I blinked at him, perplexed and surprised. His gaze was serious, so I nodded. Why ask me not to swallow? I pondered the purpose of his command while his cum rolled around in my mouth. It tasted salty and had a lumpy texture.

I couldn't speak, and I suppressed a giggle as a trickle of cum escaped my mouth. I brushed it back in with my finger before Brad noticed.

"Tilt your head back and open your mouth. I want to see your tongue swishing it around." Brad said.

I thought his request must be another teaching moment. I loved it when Brad pushed my boundaries and forced me to experience new things. I never had a man cum in my mouth and then forbid me to spit or swallow. My face flushed as I tilted my head back and carefully opened my mouth. The moment my lips parted cum bubbles dribbled out of the corners of my mouth and down my cheeks. I stopped the flow with both hands and scooped it back into my mouth. I had to tilt my head even further back to keep more from escaping because my mouth was filled almost to the brim.

I gurgled his sperm like mouthwash and wiggled my tongue around in the murky white soup. I could see his rapt expression, and it occurred to me that making a woman keep semen in her mouth must be a huge turn on for men. Whatever his motivation, I was happy to do it for him.

"Nice, now close your lips but *don't* swallow. Not until I tell you."

Trying not to laugh, I nodded carefully. I gently nudged some cum off my lips and back into my mouth before closing my lips firmly.

"Keep my cum in your mouth, and give me a strip tease. Remember, no swallowing until I tell you. Now, take off your clothes."

I liked his idea of giving me a challenge, and though my cheeks were puffed and my lips glistening with moist cum, I did my best. I had to admit that his thick globs of semen felt strange as they rolled over my tongue. The taste wasn't offensive, just a little salty and the texture was different than what I expected; almost like lumpy porridge.

The first item of clothing I removed was my black teddy. I slipped it off my shoulders and in a spirited move I tossed it at him. Brad caught it and laughed. I could see he was quickly becoming aroused again as I scooped a little squirt of semen off my lips and popped it back into my mouth. I gave him a twirl letting his eyes wander all over my body before I started to unhook my corset. I loved my corset and the way it accentuated the curves of my hips. I think Brad loved it too because it cupped my bare breasts. I peeled the corset off and bent forward, so my heavy breasts hung before his eyes. I then turned slowly and gave him a view of my ass. Every time I moved, though, I could feel his cum sloshing in my mouth, and I fought the urge to swallow. His not swallowing command was quickly becoming difficult to obey.

"Don't you dare swallow," Brad warned when he saw my concerned expression. "I think it's time you had some spankings. Go fetch your bag of sex toys like a good girl and be sure to grab the crop too."

I didn't want to fail his challenge, so I doubled my efforts to keep my lips sealed tight while I rushed to my bedroom to fetch my bondage bag. It wasn't a bondage bag really; it was just a tote bag that held all my toys, clamps and gags.

I felt like a dirty whore, and I loved it. Sometimes, in my heart, I felt like there was nothing I wouldn't let Brad do to me if it meant keeping him happy. Even penetration sex. He excited me in ways my husband never had, and I sometimes thought I would die if Brad left me. Never in a million years would I allow my husband to cum in my mouth, nor would I ever keep his cum in my mouth, forced to taste it constantly. For Brad, though, I was more than willing if it made him happy.

Returning to the living room with my bondage bag in hand, I noticed Brad had reclined on the couch. I handed him my bag of sex toys and also the riding crop then stepped back making sure to keep my head lowered and my hands at my sides. I was starting to wish he allowed me to swallow because I dearly wanted to speak, but Master was in charge, and if he commanded me not to swallow, then I would try with all my strength to obey him.

"Do you know why I'm not allowing you to swallow?" Brad asked while flexing the crop between his hands.

I shook my head trying not to giggle at how impossible it was for me to answer with words. Holding a mouthful of cum is quite an effective mouth gag, I realized. All I could do was shrug my shoulders and shake my head.

"Because I'm not happy that you are still letting your husband fuck you," Brad explained. He flicked the riding crop in the air, testing its flex. "That cum is to remind you that your body is mine. I don't mind you sucking Tim off because ultimately it makes you better at sucking me off, but I don't like his cock in your pussy. I don't care if he's your husband or not, your body belongs to me. Now, turn around and show me those cute ass cheeks of yours."

What little sex I had with my husband was bothering Brad? I was stunned. Was that jealousy I detected on his face? I liked that. It meant he hadn't tired of me yet and had no intention of ending our secret love affair. I was terrified of returning to my old life as a boring housewife.

When Brad twirled his finger, I snapped out of my thoughts and quickly turned around. I felt his warm hands caress my ass cheeks, and I smiled as best I could with his cum still rolling around in my mouth. I took the initiative and grabbed my ass cheeks and gave them a little jiggle. My ass was his and I wanted him to know it, even though we never had penetrative sex of any kind yet.

Brad had hinted on many occasions about how much he wanted to cum deep in my pussy, and I gently reminded him each time that I was fertile and young. I was quite capable of accidentally getting pregnant. That was a risk I wasn't willing to take despite how much I secretly desired it. Brad seemed mollified when I mentioned that perhaps we could try anal sex instead. Not now, though. I was wasn't ready for anal sex yet, but I knew it was constantly on his mind. Part of me wondered if all men secretly desired butt sex with women.

"Very nice, now bend over and wrap your arms around your knees and hold very still. I think I want to inspect your sweet little pussy. No swallowing. Is my cum still in your mouth?"

I glanced over my shoulder and stared at him with furrowed brows. Of course, I hadn't swallowed yet. When he saw my moist lips and puffed cheeks, he nodded with satisfaction and then placed his hand on the small of my back and gently bent me over.

I loved knowing he was looking at my pussy, inspecting it, touching it. I knew it made his cock hard. A thrill shot up my spine as I wrapped my arms around my knees. Just knowing another man had full access to my most private parts, and I couldn't do anything about it always made me wet. I couldn't speak because of the cum in my mouth so I couldn't tell him how turned on I was. I hoped when he slipped a finger into me he would be able to tell.

His hands grabbed my bent over ass cheeks roughly, and he squeezed. I loved it when he was a little rough with me. He mashed and groped each cheek and then caressed them gently before finally prying them apart. I was more exposed now, and the helpless feeling only made me feel hornier. He traced a finger around my swollen clit teasing me and then slipped it inside. I moaned as sensations exploded through my quivering pussy. I tightened my arms around my knees even more.

"Do you like having my cum in your mouth?" Brad asked in a husky voice.

I peered back and noticed his cock beginning to stir once more. I moaned and nodded as best I could. Of course, I loved his cum in my mouth, but I also really wanted to swallow it soon. The effort of keeping my lips pressed together was beginning to get uncomfortable.

"Do you want my cock inside your wet pussy?"

Sudden hesitation coursed through my brain. I wanted his cock in me more than anything, but we couldn't risk accidental pregnancy. Was his question a literal one or a fantasy question? If it was real, then no. But if his question was simply fantasy, then, of course, I wanted him to cum deep inside me. Despite the caution in my mind, I couldn't help but nod. Yes, I wanted to feel his cock in me. Part of me even wanted to have his baby.

Brad removed his wet finger from my pussy, sucked it clean and then leaned back on the couch. "If those sounds meant a yes, then reach up and pull your ass cheeks apart and hold them."

Without hesitation, I moved my hands from around my knees and grabbed handfuls my ass cheeks and pulled them apart. I gave Brad a desperate ass wiggle and wished he would finger me more. Maybe he would use a toy on me. I was so horny I might have even let him fuck my fertile pussy if he teased me much longer. I peered between my legs and looked at an upside-down image of Brad stroking his cock. He was casually gazing at my exposed sex, making me hold my cheeks apart for his viewing pleasure.

Suddenly I felt some of my wetness trail down my inner thigh. My cheeks flushed. If Brad noticed, he would comment. If he didn't fuck me soon, or use a toy, I was going to make a huge mess. Maybe he was waiting just to tease me? It didn't matter; the more aroused I became, the more I turned into putty in his hands. A few more minutes of foreplay and I would let him do whatever he wanted to me. Consequences be damned.

"I'm going to spank you for ten minutes, and then you may swallow the cum in your mouth. Do you think you can do that?"

A flood of relief filled me. I was wondering how long it would be before I could swallow. I nodded. I could handle ten more minutes.

"Good, now turn sideways and put your hands on the floor and ass in the air."

Obeying easily, I pivoted and bent forward spreading my palms on the plush carpet. I even showed a little defiance by wiggling my upturned ass. I turned my head and smiled at Brad until a little cum escaped my mouth, trailed down my chin, and hung dangling. I panicked. Would he be upset? There was nothing I could do about it. With my hands planted on the floor and my ass pushed up I couldn't scoop anything back into my mouth. Brad must have noticed, but he said nothing. I guessed the sight only added to his arousal.

The first few smacks with the crop were exploratory. Brad always started his flogging sessions this way. It didn't take long before he flicked his wrist harder and the short handled crop bit into my soft ass cheeks. I couldn't help but make a little whimper each time he struck my skin. I felt dirty and used, and it thrilled me. If he struck particularly hard with the crop, I would wiggle my ass in protest. There wasn't much else I could do. I knew he enjoyed this, and that was all that mattered to me. His pleasure was more important than my own. It was the nature of the dominant and submissive relationship we had developed, and I wouldn't have it any other way.

The worst part of being spanked by Brad was not knowing where or how hard he would strike. It could be three soft taps followed by a hard one, or two hard ones in a row and then a soft one. He knew how much I struggled not knowing the rhythm of his strokes. It was the control freak in me that he was breaking.

I would almost be relaxed, and then he would suddenly flick his wrist, and the crop would bite before I could react. The frustration was a turn on, and he loved it. I could feel my bum cheeks grow warm and knew they would be turning red under his administration. He was careful, though, never to leave any marks on my skin. Whatever redness developed always faded before my husband noticed. Tim would never think to spank me for the pure enjoyment of it like Brad did. One of the new discoveries in my life was learning that I enjoyed spankings. Who knew?

When the ten minutes were up, Brad set the crop down. I held my inverted position waiting for his next command. My ass burned, and my pussy juices had thoroughly soaked my inner thighs. I was primed and ready to be used and didn't care if he wanted to risk getting me pregnant or not. I just needed to cum. I tried to wait and be patient once the spanking was over. I even gave him little whimpering hints that I still needed to swallow. Brad massaged his wrist while gazing lazily at my dangling breasts. He seemed to be deep in thought.

"Kneel in front of me," Brad said. A full minute must have passed since he stopped flogging me and I was desperate for permission to swallow.

I unfolded from my position and knelt obediently. My ass stung a little from the crop as I rested my bottom on my feet. I could endure discomfort, though. A slave must always be willing to suffer discomfort to please her Master. I was eager to get on with the fun and hoped it didn't show on my face. Brad was just as likely to deny me pleasure to teach me a lesson. I kept my face neutral, though my cheeks were puffed out and my lips leaked more and more cum bubbles.

"You understand why I punished you?"

I nodded like a good school girl, making sure my eyes were wide and innocent.

"I don't want Tim fucking you anymore. Is that understood? You're mine."

I made a serious expression of total agreement.

"Very well then, you may swallow."

Finally!

]I swallowed hard and forced the thick gobs of cum, now mixed with my saliva, down my throat in a huge gulp. I expected to gag or at least struggle, but I didn't. Not like the first time. I felt proud. I licked my lips and opened my mouth for inspection.

"What do you say?" Brad asked with a raised eyebrow as I closed my mouth.

"Thank you, Master," I replied, finally able to speak.

"Do you want to cum?"

I tucked my hands in my lap and nodded eagerly. Part of me was excited to discover what new experience he was going to show me. Would he finally use toys on me? Perhaps I would be allowed to use the vibrator myself instead of always having him use it on me. A naughty thought filled me with anticipation; maybe he was finally going to fuck me. Whatever happened next, I knew it wouldn't be my decision. My body was his. I loved not having control. I loved being his slut-slave. My role was to wait for his decision on how and when I would cum.

"Remember a few weeks ago when you said one of your fantasies was to be fucked by a group of guys but you'd be blindfolded and have no idea who they were?" Brad asked.

Of course, I remembered. I've always dreamt of being used like a dirty whore by a bunch of male strangers, forced to pleasure them in whatever ways they desired. I've told both Brad and my husband that fantasy many times. It was the idea of being helpless that turned me on. Maybe even tied to a bed or bent over a table and strapped down. It didn't matter. The important thing was I wanted to experience not being in control; of not having any say in what happens to me sexually. I always get wet thinking of men I've never met, using my body however they want. I don't know where that fantasy came from, but I'd had it since I was a young teenager. Tim had scoffed at the idea, of course, he would never agree to group sex, or sharing me. I wondered what Brad had in mind. The idea of giving myself to strangers tweaked my curiosity.

"Yes, Master," I replied slowly.

"Good, because I have plans for you. Not today, though. Today, my little slut-slave, I want that wet little cunt of yours in the bedroom."

I smiled in delight. I loved when Brad talked dirty to me.

"Does this mean I get to orgasm, Master?"

Brad only chuckled. "That depends. Are you my dirty whore only?"

I nodded. "Yes, Master I'm *your* dirty whore."

"Are you willing to do *anything* I want?"

My pussy desperately needed an orgasm, and I nearly begged him to fuck me. What did he mean by *anything*? Was Brad referring to using toys on me or were his thoughts of something darker? The way he stressed *anything* made me feel a little nervous. Would he finally demand anal? I hoped not.

I pushed my nervousness aside. "With you, Master, I'm willing to try anything," I confessed.

I was growing to love and trust Brad, and I enjoyed our secret sessions. I just had to get over my nervousness whenever he pushed my limits and made me grow. I wanted to be his submissive woman. Brad had changed my life and revitalized my sex drive. I couldn't go back to the way my life was before. I won't go back. I had no choice but follow the path Brad is leading me down if I want to experience it all. Part of me suspected Brad knew that and was grooming me to be what I was now. I am grateful none-the-less. Inch by inch my body is slowly becoming Brad's to use as he sees fit. It's only a matter of time until he fucks me. I noticed his grin as he watched me thinking. I smirked slightly and gave him my most alluring naughty smile.

"Get that hot naked body of yours on the bed. I'm not done playing before your husband gets home."

"Yes, Master," I said and scurried like a good slut-slave should.

I eagerly climbed onto my bed and waited for Brad who strolled into my bedroom like he owned my house. He was so full of confidence. I could see his eyes travel up and down my naked body. I always felt thrills knowing my body aroused him. I loved the way he looked at me as I waited on the bed while he stroked his hard cock. I wished my husband appreciated me like Brad did instead of taking me for granted. None of this would ever have happened if Tim showered me with the attention Brad did. No matter, I have a secret lover, and he took care of all my needs instead.

"What would Master like his little slut-slave to do?" I asked.

"Lay on your back, and press those big juicy tits together," Brad commanded in his no-nonsense voice.

"When will Slave be allowed to orgasm?" I press him. I know I'm skirting the rules as a submissive by thinking of myself, so I used my most innocent voice. I'm very horny and wanted to remind him that I hadn't cummed yet.

He frowned as he straddled my torso. I watched as he stroked his cock above my waiting body. I was completely at his mercy.

"Slave must remember her place," Brad said in a conversational tone. I tensed, hoping he didn't decide on giving me more punishment. "Slave doesn't cum until Master decides. Do you forget the rules so easily, slut?"

I shook my head. "No, Master. Forgive Slave for thinking of her desires and not Master's desires."

"Much better. Now press those big tits together for me."

I obey and cupped my breasts in my hands and mash them together. Brad leaned forward and placed his cock on my face. I opened my lips, and he inserted himself roughly. I tried my best to get his cock nice and wet with my saliva, darting my tongue around his hard shaft while he relaxed and let my mouth pleasure him. He then pulled his wet cock out of my mouth and slipped it between my pushed together breasts, penetrating my tight cleavage.

He grabbed the headboard and leaned forward while I adjusted my hands to push my breasts together harder. He began to hump my chest, and I looked up, hoping my face was submissive and innocent.

I wanted to cum badly, but he was right, I should be a good slut-slave and think of his needs first. Sometimes I think I have so much still to learn about being a submissive. He will decide when I orgasm, and I need to leave that decision in his hands no matter how aroused I become. He quickened his pace, and I felt my body pushed into the mattress with each powerful thrust. My cleavage warmed from the friction of his cock; the soft white skin turned a reddish hue. Despite the slight discomfort, I held my tits firmly around his cock and waited patiently as he enjoyed himself. That's all that mattered to me.

"Do you want me to cum inside you?" Brad asked between thrusts.

I adjusted my hands again keeping my breasts together and nod tentatively as I softly bit my lip. I didn't know if this was more dirty talk or a real question.

"Yes, Master." I locked eyes with him. "I want that more than anything."

My answer must have aroused him, and he increased his hip thrusts, forcing his hard cock between my breasts even faster. I know Brad liked to hear me talk dirty. How many times did he masturbate while listening to my voice read him a dirty story? I know if I keep pleasing him, I might be permitted to orgasm.

"How about anal? Would you like to try that, Julie?"

I moan and nod as if anal was my deepest desire. "Yes, Master, anytime you desire it, but only if it's your cock in my ass, not my husband's cock. My only wish is to please you, Master."

"Tell me your ass is mine."

"My ass is yours, Master," I breathe heavily. My cleavage burns.

His pace quickened. He closed his eyes, and I knew he is enjoying the tightness of my squeezed breasts. I felt dirty and used. He was taking pleasure only for himself and giving me none, as was his prerogative as Dom. It made my pussy ache to cum, though.

"Why did you never let your husband fuck you in the ass?"

I thought for a moment. "My husband begs for it all the time, Master, but I know my body belongs only to you. I will never let him in there. I'm saving that special place for you, Master. Whenever you want it, you can put it in there, but know that your slave is nervous."

My words have the desired effect. Brad groans and continues his merciless humping. I can feel the soft skin between my breasts becoming very irritated from the friction. I started to feel a little pain, but I endured it patiently. His pleasure was my only focus.

"Which would you rather have, my cock in your pussy or your ass?"

I felt a thrill of anticipation but also apprehension about getting pregnant and my husband discovering my torrid love affair. I felt conflicted. While holding my breasts as Brad fucked them, I thought about the best answer. I wanted him to cum inside me, and I had to admit the possibility of having Brad's baby was a huge turn on for me. I also knew Brad wanted to try anal on me, but anal scared me. In every anal video I had seen, it looked very painful.

"Whatever Master wishes," I answered, deciding to let Brad make the decision for me. If he wanted to cum in my fertile pussy, I would let him. I couldn't resist the temptation any longer. On the other hand, if he wanted to fuck my butt, I would endure the pain and discomfort for him too. I just hoped he was gentle.

Brad leaned back and grabbed his cock. I watched with helpless curiosity as he aimed his cock at my face while jerking off. Should my mouth be open? I don't know. He never gave me a command, so I simply watched him stroke himself. He concentrated and then grunted. I felt his hot cum blast my face without warning, hitting me in the eye. I flinched again and closed both my eyes and my mouth. A wad of cum hit my nose then another across my lips. More trails across my forehead and sails into my hair. I held still knowing he liked to hit various parts of my face with his semen. I felt some warm droplets land on my cheek and neck. He didn't ejaculate much the second time; he never does, but it was always more than Tim ever managed, even on his best day.

I held very still, feeling his cum cool on my soft skin. I couldn't imagine what my face looked like splattered with semen, but I knew he liked it. I smiled and waited with my eyes closed, content that I gave him pleasure. Sometimes he made me wait a long time with my face plastered while he enjoyed the sight or snapped pictures.

"Open your mouth," I heard him say.

I obeyed. Brad slipped his spent cock between my lips, and I started to suckle it gently. He liked it when I cleaned his cock. I would never do that for my husband. When Brad was satisfied, he pulled his clean cock from my mouth and tucked it away. I closed my mouth and swallowed as I waited for his next command. Part of me felt disappointed that he had two orgasms already while I hadn't had any, but his needs come first. Another part of me was also disappointed that he didn't cum inside my pussy.

He climbed off of my torso, and I heard him pulling tissues from the box. A moment later he stuffed them in my hand. I sat up, unwilling to open my eyes until I cleaned his semen off my lids.

"Clean yourself up. No orgasm for you today."

What? I was crestfallen, and my face showed it. I quickly scooped his congealed cum from my eyes to looked at him, but he had already left the room. I think to call after him, but once Master has decided something, I can never dissuade him. My hesitation costs me. I heard the front door close. He was gone before I even cleaned my face. Just like that, I'm left alone, in bewildered silence.

I rolled out of bed and stumbled to the front door. I watched as Brad's little red car disappeared around the corner and I suddenly felt like crying. What had I done wrong? Why did he leave so abruptly? I stared in dismay, hoping he would come back, but he didn't. Did I offend him? I'm truly at a loss. I sadly walked to the bathroom and peered at myself in the mirror. There was cum splattered all over my face and hair. I hated spooge in my hair; it was so difficult to get out.

I turned on the shower and made it nice and warm. I had no time to wallow in my self-pity. I had to clean up the bedroom, and then hide my bondage bag and make sure there was no evidence my husband could find. Brad never helped me with cleaning up after our sessions. It was below him. Besides, he taught me that submissives cleaned up, not dominants.

My heart ached, though. I felt used. I was hoping for a little snuggle time with Brad, but that possibility was gone. Was denying me an orgasm, Brad's way of showing his displeasure that my husband had sex with me the other night? Brad wanted total control over my body and my sex life even though I was married.

By the time I've showered and cleaned, there is an email on my tablet from Brad. His instruction was terse and to the point:

Meet me at the Riverview Strip Club this Friday at ten o'clock. I have a surprise planned. Bring your bondage bag and lingerie.

I read his email again and wondered if he meant ten in the morning or ten at night. A quick internet search doesn't reveal the strip club hours. The next question in my mind was why a strip club? Was I supposed to bring my bondage bag and lingerie to a strip club? Whatever for?

Perplexed, I decided to get clarification. He already seemed upset enough to deny me an orgasm, so I might as well further annoy him and ask for more details. If I was going to obey his commands, then I needed to know if he meant morning or night. I had to get away from the house without raising my husband's suspicions. If Brad was upset by my asking, then that's not my problem. He should have been more specific. I type a quick reply:

Please clarify, Master. Ten in the morning or at night? Slave wishes to obey.

I waited five minutes, but there was no reply. I still ached for an orgasm and was tempted say *fuck-it-all* and go back to my bedroom and use my vibrator. I glance at the wall clock. Hubby and monkey-boy should be back in a few hours.

My tablet dinged. I opened my email and read:

Ten in the morning. You will do this, no questions asked. Master.

A hundred different questions flood my mind. Brad knew how much I liked to be in control and how I struggled not knowing the details of things ahead of time. I was sure he purposely gave me very little information so my mind would spin. I calmed my fluttering heart and focused my thoughts.

I type a quick reply: *Slave will obey.*

I folded my arms and pouted. For the life of me, I couldn't fathom his reason for me to show up at a strip club with my bondage bag and lingerie. Why a strip club? And why in the morning? Am I to perform on stage? Hardly. As high school teachers, someone could easily spot either of us and report it to the Board Office. It would mean the end of our careers. No I won't be stripping, even if he asked me, I wouldn't do it. I would use my safe word or flat out refuse. It's far too risky. Besides, even without the risk of someone in the public recognizing a school teacher stripping, Brad knows how uncoordinated I am. The last thing he wanted to see was me floundering on a dance stage or breaking my arm falling off a stripper pole. Whatever his reason, I was left mystified.

I could almost imagine Brad chuckling to himself knowing how my mind worked in this kind of situation. This secret rendezvous would have been something he planned carefully, and secretly, well in advance. For once, his motive completely escapes me. At least I'll have all week to think about it unless I can pry it out of him sooner. Part of me thought that wouldn't be likely.

* * *

As it turned out, I found his command not to have sex with my husband, more difficult to follow than I first anticipated. By the third day of coming up with creative ways to deny my husband sex, I was running out of ideas. There were only so many times the 'I have a headache' routine works.

I finally told my husband just to watch porn on the computer and rub one out. He seemed mollified, at least, but I knew it would keep his paws off me for a few days. I felt some pangs of guilt-denying the man I married access to my body, but it was important that I fully explored the world of submission Brad had opened for me. I might have broken my marital vows, but I wasn't going to break my obedience vows to Master.

The excuse I made for leaving early on Friday was an easy lie. I told Tim I was meeting up with one of my girlfriends from college for a few hours and that we might go out for wings. He barely grunted and promised to feed our son lunch while I was gone. How nice of him, I thought.

I discreetly packed my bondage bag out of sight in the van. I also tucked a few extra lingerie outfits into my purse just in case Master didn't like any particular one. It would be good to have options and offer him alternatives. A good submissive always anticipates her Master's desires. Because my cover story was meeting an old friend for drinks, I didn't raise any suspicions in my husband's eyes when I added a little makeup and mascara before heading out. I hugged my son and waved at Tim before I jumped in the van and drove to the strip club.

I was still perplexed about what Brad's motivation and I had thoroughly exhausted every plausible scenario in my mind without success. During the week his anger seemed to simmer once I promised him that my husband was completely cut off. I had hoped to pry some hints about our Friday rendezvous, but Brad wouldn't even drop a hint. All I knew was if he had spent this much time planning something, then it must be good.

The strip club was in the industrial part of the city, tucked between factories and storage buildings, and also near the deli sandwich shop Brad loved. Despite the early hour, I was surprised to see cars parked in their lot. I hoped to find Brad's little red car, and when I spotted it, I parked my van as close as possible. Taking a deep breath, I calmed my nerves and then grabbed my bondage bag and purse.

This was it.

My heart was racing, and I suddenly had doubts about the wisdom of what I was about to do. I had never been inside a strip club. I looked at Brad's car as if it's very presence would give me courage. It didn't. I reasoned, that if Brad were inside the club, then everything would be okay. I swallowed hard and got out of my van. I had butterflies in my tummy, and even my knees felt wobbly. This was by far the most risqué thing I had ever done. I glanced around hoping no one would recognize me and then power-walked towards the club entrance.

The dim interior of the club felt gloomy and smelled of stale cigarettes and carpet cleaner. I stood and waited for my eyes to adjust as the heavy door closed behind me. I was certain the thumping of my heart would reverberate off the walls.

So this is what a strip club looks like on the inside? The place was empty except for the bartender, who stood behind a long serving area in front of a wall of just about every liquor bottle known to humanity. The bartender looked up from his newspaper and glanced at me for a moment before returning his reading. *Friendly fellow.*

I looked around. The main stage jutted into a sea of tables and chairs. That was where the girls took off their clothes, I guessed. It surprised me how close the patrons sat at the edge of the stage, but then again, I had never been to a strip club, so

I had no idea what was normal. A shiny brass floor-to-ceiling pole was the only prop on the otherwise black runway. I peered at the empty DJ booth and wondered where all the people were. I guessed patrons didn't enjoy strip clubs this early in the morning, or perhaps the place wasn't even open yet. That didn't explain why there were so many cars parked outside or why Brad had requested my presence along with my bondage bag and lingerie. At least it appeared I wouldn't be stripping for an audience. What a relief.

I approached the bartender, but he forestalled my questions by pointing towards the stage without looking up. "Through the curtains," he said.

"Thank you," I said politely.

Turning, I clutched my bondage bag and purse and made my way towards the stage. There was a small set of steps which I climbed, my high heel shoes clacking as I went. Once I was on the stage, I turned and peered back at the empty tables and chairs. Bright light fixtures mounted on the ceiling blinded me from seeing anything but the nearest tables. I wondered if that was how the women dealt with so many leering eyes. I wasn't sure I could strip for total strangers but being partially blinded might help.

I parted the curtains and nearly stumbled into an equally surprised woman coming the other way. She was wearing a gold-colored bikini covered in dazzling tassels, and her face was perfected with makeup. Her bright blue eyes were what startled me the most about the woman. She was stunning, and I immediately assumed she was one of the strippers.

"I'm sorry," I blurted trying to make my apologies for nearly bowling the woman over. But the other woman wasn't offended. In fact, the woman smiled.

"You must be Julie."

I blinked in surprise. "That's right, hello. I was supposed to be here—"

"At ten, yes. We were expecting you. Hello, my name is Brittney." She extended her hand.

I instantly liked Brittney and shook her offered hand. "Are you a stripper?"

Brittney laughed. "Oh, god no. And they call them exotic dancers, dear. No, I'm not a stripper. I'm a submissive like you. I was ordered by my Master to wait by the door for your arrival. Please, come with me I'll help you get changed."

"Changed? What's going on here?" I asked hoping to pry some information out of the beautiful woman. She winked and motioned me to follow her. I had no other options, so I let her lead.

She brought me to a set of stairs leading to the basement before turning briefly and giving me a smile. I followed her down the steps, thinking I had no idea strip clubs even had basements. At the bottom of the stairs, she paused and gave me a reassuring smile again and then knocked on a black door.

A viewport in the door slid opened, and a face peered out, looking first at Brittney and then at me. Then the viewport closed. I could hear latches and locks being unlatched and unlocked and I wondered once again what sort of place I was entering? Why did they lock their basement door with so much security? Was I about to be kidnapped or something? I glanced at Brittney, but she seemed perfectly calm. I also knew Brad's car was outside, and I hadn't spotted him upstairs, so reason told me he was probably on the other side of the door as well. I tried to take solace, but I couldn't help but feel apprehensive. My experience so far was way outside of my comfort zone, but I had to trust Brad wouldn't do something untoward. He must have had a very specific plan for me to justify all these hoops I had to jump through. I just hoped it was all worth it.

The door opened, and I gazed at a very large muscular man. He didn't smile. Brittney breezed past him, and I quickly followed suit. The brute shut the door, and I peeked back at the array of locks and bolts he started to put back in place. I didn't feel like I was in a basement so much as a vault. Or a dungeon. My heart was racing again. Where the hell was Brad? I could see walk-in refrigerators and stacks of beer cases along the wall. That wouldn't justify such a fortified door or the presence of a giant guard. Where was I?

"Brittney, what are we doing here?" My voice sounded small in my ears.

She slowed to a stop, her bright blue eyes glanced around before they finally settled on me. Her face became concerned and she placed a hand on my shoulder.

"You mean you don't know?"

I shook my head. Of course not, that's why I was asking.

"If your Dom didn't tell you, then I'm not sure it's my place to reveal that information to you. All I can say is you're the entertainment, and everyone is very excited to see you."

"I'm the entertainment?" I asked. What the hell was that supposed to mean?

She slipped her hand into mine and gave it a comforting squeeze. "Come on you need to get changed. I'll help you with your makeup. We need to hurry, they don't like waiting, especially for a new girl."

I had more questions, but Brittney wasn't going to give me any details. I clutched my bondage bag and purse and followed her around the stacks of beer and the refrigerators to yet another door. How many levels did they have in this place? Brittney pushed the door open, and we descended a flight of concrete stairs. At the bottom, there was a long hallway. She led me down the corridor and through a side door and into what appeared to be a change room.

"This is quite the place," I observed hoping Brittney would offer more information. She only smiled and pointed to a short wooden bench.

"Let's see what kind of lingerie you brought. If you don't have any, don't worry, we have a selection here you can choose from," Brittney said.

"I brought my own," I said. I opened my purse and pulled out my neatly folded outfits, and Brittney's eyes brightened.

"Oh god these are nice. Now, let's see what we have here," she said while unfolding my unmentionables and inspecting them. "Very nice, oh this one is expensive. Not bad. You have good taste in lingerie."

"Thank you, they were gifts from Brad," I said. I didn't mention that my husband never bought me lingerie.

"A word of advice," Brittney said as she stopped inspecting my items and looked at me. "From here on in don't refer to your Dom by name. Call Brad, or any male, Master or simply, Sir. From what I've heard of Brad, he isn't the kind of man you want to humiliate."

I perked up. Did she know Brad? "What do you mean? How do you know him? What have you heard about him?"

Brittney only smiled. She selected a pink and white school girl costume and handed it to me. "Put this on and I'll do your makeup."

Feeling more confused than ever I began to undress. Brittney fussed with the makeup, selecting the colors and hues she would apply. I was perfectly capable of putting on my own makeup, but it seemed Brittney had been instructed to take charge, so I quietly dressed in the clothes she chose. I liked my school girl outfit. It had a clip on collar and stubby pink tie, and also a plunging neckline that accented my cleavage in a flattering manner. The sides were lace, with drawstrings to cinch it around my waist. The second half of the school girl outfit was a pink and black plaid miniskirt that barely covered my ass cheeks.

"Should I wear my white garter stockings?" I asked pulling them out of my purse and holding them up for Brittney to inspect.

She turned and smiled when she saw them. "Oh yes, those are really nice. Crotchless? Good. No panties or bra, though. Just put on that outfit and the stockings. You're going to look so fucking hot."

I blushed at her compliment, but I didn't know why. Perhaps it was her enthusiasm that I would look hot. No one had told me I was hot in a very long time. I sat on the bench and rolled the stocking up my tone legs. The stockings ended mid-thigh and then white lace straps continued until they met the frilly elastic band that went around my waist. I felt sexy in those stockings, and I liked that they were crotchless.

When I was, I stood and gave Brittney a twirl. She seemed happy and gestured towards the chair in front of a large illuminated mirror and a table covered in an array of makeup. I looked at myself in the mirror while she took a position behind me. I did look hot, I thought. Brittney divided my long dark hair into pigtails, and I giggled. I would never have thought to put my hair in pigtails, but after seeing the effect in the mirror, I decided they did make me look cute.

Next, she selected bright pink lipstick and applied it to my lips. I could tell right away she had considerable skill in applying makeup. I wondered if she was a makeup artist professionally but I didn't ask. She touched my cheeks with blush and then spritzed me with a dab of perfume. I liked the smell; it was fruity with a hint of musk. I imagined it was something a teenage girl would wear on a date.

"There, all done," Brittney said as she stood back and admired her work.

I looked at her in the mirror. "What about my eyes?"

"You won't need any eye makeup because you'll be wearing this," Brittney said holding up a blindfold.

She must have seen my surprise. "They always blindfold new girls. But before I put this on, I have to tape your eyes closed first. But don't worry it won't hurt to remove later. They use special medical tape as an added precaution against peeking. I had the same thing done to me, my first time here."

I didn't know what to say. "You're going to tape my eyes shut and then blindfold me? What's going to happen to me?"

"I explained before that I am not permitted to say. Let me apply the tape and the blindfold and then I'll lead you to your Dom. Don't be afraid. This preparation is just part of the experience," Brittney explained. "All the girls go through this their first times here. It's perfectly normal to be nervous."

She waited a moment while I adjusted to the idea of wearing a blindfold. I glanced at the blindfold and the roll of medical tape and swallowed my courage and then looked her in the eye. "I'm trusting you."

"You'll be fine. I've read in a magazine that when you cannot see, your other senses become more acute. You are going to have a wonderful experience. Ride the wave, Julie.

What is about to happen to you is a very rare opportunity, and you should be thankful for being given it."

I didn't feel thankful. I didn't know what to expect, so how could I be thankful? I nodded, though, just to be safe. Brittney leaned close, and I watched her gently tear off little strips of medical tape. She leaned closer, and I closed my eyes. I could feel the tape sealing my eyelids shut and fought the urge to bolt out of my chair. After Brittney had applied the last piece of tape over my eyes, she slipped the blindfold over my face and secured the strap under my pigtails, drawing it snug.

"Can you see?"

"You're joking, right?" I was in complete darkness.

I felt Brittney's hand on my own. "Just relax, I will lead you."

"So, it's normal to be afraid you said?"

I could hear Brittney laugh. I hadn't noticed before, but she had a beautiful laugh, rich and pure. Maybe she was right; with your sight removed, maybe your other senses were heightened.

"Oh gosh!" Brittney suddenly cried.

I started and nearly jumped. "What? What's wrong?"

"I'm sorry I forgot your high heels, dear. That would have been unforgivable. Here, don't move, I will put them on you."

She was right; I could feel the cool floor through my white stocking feet. I felt her hands on my calf muscles as she supported my leg. I bent slightly forward and placed my hand on her shoulder for support. Brittney didn't say a word as she slipped heels onto my feet. I wanted to ask what color the heels were, but I could sense her unease, so I remained quiet. Once Brittney had fastened the last buckle, I felt her hand on mine, and I stood on uncertain legs.

"Wow these are very high heels," I commented feeling all my weight transfer to the balls of my feet. As a teacher, I was accustomed to wearing heels, but these stilettos took some getting used to.

"Wow they look great," Brittney said. I felt her hand on my leg again, but this time, it was caressing. "Your calf muscles form into nice little balls. You clean up nicely. They're going to love you. Okay, let's go."

I nodded and felt her lead me out of the change room. For some reason, my pussy felt warm. Was I getting aroused from her touch? The tape over my eyes prevented even a little peeking through the bottom of my blindfold. The idea of losing control and being helpless probably made me aroused, not her touch. I was completely at her mercy, but every step was sure, and I didn't stumble. After a short walk, I felt her stop me.

"We are just outside the room now," Brittney said. "Stand here and don't move. Remember, no talking unless asked a question and then be sure you answer promptly. Don't forget to be obedient. You're a very lucky woman. Not many girls ever get this experience. I almost envy you."

Almost? I felt her hand leave my own and could hear a doc being opened and then closed. I stood in silence, my hands clutched in front of me, wearing my pink and white school girl outfit, crotchless white stockings, stiletto heels and pigtails, I felt vulnerable. My world was completely dark. My heart was racing too. I longed to hear the safety of Brad's voice.

Without being able to look at a clock, I had no idea how long I waited outside the door. It could have been ten minutes; it could have been twenty. My feet started to ache a little from the uncomfortable stilettos. I wanted to lean against the wall or sit down, but I had no idea what was around me and didn't want to crash to the floor.

When the door suddenly opened, I listened very carefully. Was that Brad? The door closed, and then there was silence. Someone was there. I could hear breathing. I felt a hand caress the side of my face, and I flinched; not out of fear but because I wasn't expecting it. It felt like a man's hand, large and strong. I wanted to speak, and ask if the person was Brad, but Brittney's warning, fresh in my mind kept my voice still.

The caressing hand vanished from my face, and a moment later I felt the back of my skirt move which exposed my bum cheeks. The hand then touched my bottom, causing my heart to flutter. I bit my lip and remained submissive and still. The hand slid across my ass before roaming up and down. It then slowed to a stop and grabbed a handful of cheek. I felt the second hand as it slipped down the front of my school girl outfit and cupped my breast. They were strong male hands. My heart raced even harder, and my breathing quickened. I remained motionless as by body was casually groped. Was it Brad groping me or was it a stranger taking liberties? My pussy tingled at the thought of someone I didn't even know, touching my body as they pleased.

I was startled by strong hands grabbing my wrists. Something cold and hard pressed against my skin followed by the sound of cinching handcuffs. A small gasp of surprise had escaped my lips before I clamped my mouth shut. Every fiber of my body wanted to speak and ask what was happening. I wanted some control, but I fought the urge and remained silent. I had to be submissive. A feeling of complete helplessness washed over me, and I grew more aroused.

Whoever was beside me, wasn't speaking. I felt my cuffed wrists being pulled as I was lead to the door. I stumbled at first, caught both off guard and off balance, but I managed to regain my footing in my heels. I was in complete darkness, and I couldn't hear a sound other than my stilettos clicking on the hard floor.

Was Brad leading me or was he sitting somewhere and watching me? How many people were looking at me? I had no idea. I wanted to know and struggled with being unable to find out. I simply let whoever was holding my cuffed wrists lead me. He stopped, and I stopped.

I felt something fastened to my handcuffs, but I didn't know what it was. To my right was a sound like a boat winch, and I tilted my head to listen. The sound reminded me of times I had seen large boats hauled out of the water as a child. Chains were moving and clanking. A moment later I felt my cuffed wrists slowly rise over my head. The cranking sound stopped just before the tips of my toes were about to leave the ground. I felt stretched and vulnerable and had no idea what was happening. I tried to remain calm as I chewed my lip. So far nothing bad had happened to me other than a little mysterious groping. I reminded myself that I had to remain submissive and not struggle or complain. Brittney had said she was bringing me to see Brad. He had to be close. I took solace in that.

There was someone behind me. I could feel a hard body press against my own. Strong hands ran up my sides and then across my chest where they cupped my breasts through my outfit. I felt vulnerable and intimate at the same time. It was an odd feeling. The hands groped me roughly and then I felt them grab the plunging neckline of my school girl outfit. I could feel hands bunching the fabric and then quite suddenly, yank it apart. There was a tearing sound at first as tiny threads snapped and then a louder sound as the entire front of my outfit was ripped in two releasing my bare breasts for all to see.

I gasped with a mixture of shock and dismay. *My outfit was ruined!* The strong hands released the tattered remains of my top and scooped my heavy breasts. I could feel my boobs being juggled up and down for all to see. A murmur of mild applause and a chorus of murmuring male voices filled the air. There were people in front of me watching. I felt both mortified and exhilarated at the same time. Until now, only Brad and my husband had seen my bare breasts. But now they were freely on display for unknown strangers. Knowing men were watching my debasement somehow spiked my sexual arousal quicker than anything I had experienced in my life. I

113

liked the thrill of being made so helpless. Just knowing men were looking at my breasts, and there was nothing I could do to stop them made my pussy throb with desire. Were they good looking men? Maybe they were fat hairy men? I hoped not, but I had no idea. Part of the thrill was not knowing.

My miniskirt was yanked down my legs to my ankles. I obediently stepped out of them. I didn't want those torn by Mr. Muscles. Strong hands forced my legs apart, and I gasped. I felt more cold metal around each ankle and realized they were putting a spreader bar on me. I had learned about that device during one of Brad's lessons where he had me name various bondage items in a picture. When the spreader bar was attached, I hung from my cuffs, the metal painfully digging into my wrists. Someone lowered the pulley chain until my spread legs once more touched the ground. With crotchless stockings and no panties on I knew anyone crouching in front of me could get a very close and personal view of my wet pussy, and I would never know. Was someone peering at my privates right now? I suddenly understood the reason for taping my eyes shut. I couldn't even peek out of the bottom of my blindfold.

Tensing, I waited for the next thing to happen to me, but nothing did. No one groped me or attached anything to my body. I heard whoever was near me walk away, leaving me bound and secured in total darkness. I knew Brad and Brittney were probably looking at me, or were at least nearby, but I had no idea who else was there or how many. I heard voices, though, low pitched and though I strained my ears I could make nothing out.

The cool air from an air conditioning vent kept my nipples hard and dotted my sides with goosebumps. I moved my head back and forth trying to stretch my shoulders. I still wore my white crotchless stockings and stiletto heels, but my school girl outfit was ruined beyond repair. I felt as helpless as a person could and yet I wasn't afraid. My pussy had to be very wet, and I yearned to pleasure myself, but I couldn't. I could feel a warmth spreading through my bound body. There was something both mysterious and thrilling about strangers seeing me sexually vulnerable and at their mercy. Brad must have arranged for men to watch my humiliation. He knew what a powerful fantasy this was for me.

"How are you holding up?" A soft voice startled me.

Brad! I lifted my head and turned towards the sound but before I could speak he cautioned me to whisper.

"I'm a bit nervous. Should I call you Master? What's happening?"

"They are continuing with their meeting and taking a break. I just came up to see how you were doing."

"What meeting? Who are these men? What's going on, Brad?"

"You're at a bondage club meeting, and they are evaluating whether or not to let us join. What is happening now is partially an inspection and partially an initiation. If things go well, then both of us will be accepted into their club."

I was flabbergasted. "Shouldn't you have asked me first?"

Brad chuckled. "It never occurred to me. Joining this club will open up doors for both of us and accelerate your training."

"Well, this is still unexpected," I stammered, trying to think of an argument. I didn't like Brad's casual tone, but he was my Dom, and I had to trust his judgment. That didn't mean I had to like it, even though I did. He should have asked me first if I wanted this.

I felt Brad's hand cup my breast, and I smiled. I wished the damned blindfold was off so I could at least see his face. I moaned as he found my hard nipple and rolled it between his fingers.

"Is Pet starting to feel better?"

I smiled and nodded like an obedient schoolgirl.

"I want you to enjoy yourself. This club is a very exclusive group of very important people. Will you do this for me, my love?" Brad whispered. His hand slipped across to my other breast playing me like putty.

I liked the sound of his voice. Part of me was compelled to please him because I wanted our relationship to continue. Another part of me was out of my element, though, and I was more than a little nervous still. I had never dreamt I would experience anything like this with my husband. If I gave up now, would I have to go back to my old life? Probably. I wanted to see where this path took me. If I gave up now, I might spend the rest of my life wondering, *what if.*

"I will do this for you, Master. But I'm scared. Please tell me you love me."

His hand left my breast. I smiled, waiting in anticipation for his words and maybe a kiss. I needed to know that he loved me. I tilted my head, but there were no words. There was nothing.

"Brad?"

There was no reply.

"Master?" I whispered the word louder.

Still nothing. Had he heard my question? I didn't know, but I hoped he had. Alone once more, I waited. My arms were becoming tired of being strung over my head. I remembered reading that it takes months and even years of training to be able to endure tight bondage poses for any length of time. My tolerance for being tightly bound was barely above neophyte level. I hated being in the dark, and I hated not knowing what was about to happen to me. Brad knew I always struggled with surrendering especially without knowing all the details first. Perhaps that was why he kept everything secret and never asked my opinion. I could only imagine his amusement as he sat in a chair watching me.

I lost track of time once again. Had ten minutes passed? Twenty? The mysterious men and Brad seemed perfectly content with leaving me bound and helpless while they talked. I didn't even know they had bondage clubs. Why would I even want to join a bondage club? Was it like Scouts where you get badges for being tied in different ways? I hated making difficult decisions based on little information. So why was I trying to join a group I knew nothing about?

Because Brad wanted us to.

I thought they could have had their meeting by themselves and saved me a lot of aggravation and stress. It's was a very strange feeling to be treated like nothing more than an object. I wasn't a person who required politeness or attention, or even a thank you. No, I was simply something to be used at a whim and then left. Maybe that was part of the test. Sneaky. I knew I should be angry and offended, but within the boundaries of fantasy, I was wet and horny for more abuse. With nothing to do but wait, I tried guessing what was about to happen. Speculation, at least, helped pass the time.

The talking had stopped for a while before my brain registered the silence. I held very still and listened. I heard chairs moving. Something was happening. The men were now taking their seats for the show. My body tensed.

I heard the click clack of high heels approaching from my left, and I cocked my head. A female was approaching me, and I hoped it was Brittney. I felt a soft, cool hand on my breast a moment later. It was a female hand.

"Just relax and enjoy," I heard Brittney whisper in my ear as she caressed my neck and cupped one of my breasts. A woman had never touched my breasts before. Her touch was quite different from the way I was used to. She was gentle and her touch light, almost like grazing fingertips that sent tingles through me.

I wondered if I should risk asking a question.

"The men are all watching you now," Brittney continued.

"How many?" I whispered, but her reply was a soft musical giggle.

Brittney's grazing caress felt amazing on my bare skin. I smiled as she gently traced the curves of each breast. But the smile was short-lived. Without warning, Brittney pinched each of my nipples painfully and lifted my breasts off my chest and held them suspended. No one had ever done that to me before, and I gasped. The weight of my heavy breasts tented my nipples and sent pain shooting through my chest. The pleasurable feeling of her earlier caressing was gone. Replaced now by sharp pain. My obvious discomfort had no effect on Brittney. She pinched my nipples harder and began to bob her hands up and down like my breasts were bouncy toys to be played with. I was helpless to stop her.

I wanted to cry in pain or at least beg her to be gentle, but I recalled Brad's words that this was an evaluation. If I complained then the mystery men watching me would take notice. Perhaps they were looking to see how well I endured the pain? If I cried, perhaps our membership would be denied? I closed my lips and endured the humiliation and pain of my tormented breasts.

After a few minutes, Brittney stopped her arm movements but held my nipples firmly pinched between her fingers. She slowly pulled them upward lifting my breasts off my chest once more. She kept pulling until my breasts could go no higher and the soft underside was exposed. She then pulled some more, stretching my nipples as far as they would go and causing my face to contort. Then she held stopped and waited. I whimpered and tried to lift my body higher on my toes to relieve the pain, but Brittney just pulled my breasts higher to compensate. I had to remain now on my toes as well as endure the sharp pains shooting through my chest. I had no idea how long she would make me endure the pain. After what seemed like an hour, but was probably only a minute or two, she suddenly released my stretched nipples and let my boobs fall back into place. I knew the men watching must have enjoyed my suffering, but I didn't care. All my focus was on ignoring the searing pain radiating around my breasts. My nipples felt stretched and tender. I made a mental note to someday return the favor and see how Brittney liked it.

Next, I suddenly felt her warm mouth sucking each nipple. I tensed at first, but her mouth felt good, and I moaned. She moved her mouth from side to side sucking and gently kissing each breast until I had relaxed. The pain was still there, radiating across my chest but at least she had dulled it a little. When she stopped, I knew my tender nipples had to be fully erect and puffy for everyone to see.

My soothing relief was short-lived. Something hard and metallic bit my nipple without warning, making me gasp in shock. I heard the tinkle of a chain, and then my other nipple was bitten as well.

Nipple clamps!

Now I knew the reason why Brittney pulled and bounced my breasts so roughly; she wanted to get my nipples as large as possible.

"Tilt your head down and open your mouth." It was Brittney's voice.

I obeyed and felt a thin chain placed between my lips. I closed my teeth over the chain instinctively and waited.

"Now lift your head and keep your chin up. If you lower your head, even slightly, then these beautiful tits will are going to feel my whip."

Yikes. I nodded and lifted my head, feeling my nipples cry in protest.

"Further."

I lifted my chin higher and felt the weight of my breasts start to tent my nipples as I pulled. I wasn't sure how long I could hold this position, and I could only imagine what it must look like to the men watching me.

I felt Brittney's hands start to caress my body, and I had to admit the sensations were pleasant, contrasting with the pain in my breasts. When she reached my bare ass cheeks, Brittney spun me on the suspended chain, so my backside was now facing the men. I felt my face flush knowing complete strangers could now see my bare bottom.

A moment later I felt the unmistakable slap of a paddle strike my ass. I was caught so completely off guard that I cried out in shock. Pain radiated across my bottom. Another strike made me flinch and clench my ass cheeks. Whoever was spanking me with that paddle had no qualms about hitting hard.

"Keep that head up."

I lifted my sagging head and winced. Two more slaps from the paddle connected hard on each butt cheek, and I writhed and contorted my body as best I could with suspended arms and toes that barely touched the floor. I wasn't able to escape, though, and another whack was followed in succession by four or five quick paddles in a row. I gasped and whimpered and finally cried in pain. I had been spanked before by Brad, but he used his hand and a small crop and never really struck me hard. This experience was something new. I was being hit by a wide flat paddle that made my entire ass jiggle and left large red patches on my smooth cheeks.

There was a pause, and I hung my head in shame. My ass throbbed and stung all over. Was my spanking over? I didn't know. I desperately wanted to rub my sore bottom but I couldn't. I felt helpless with my arms above my head, and my legs spread apart, barely touching to ground.

"Do you guys want to see her spanked some more?" Brittney asked the audience. There was a chorus of cheers. Brittney spun me around by my wrists until I was facing the men.

I whimpered in pain.

"What would you like?" Brittney asked the crowd. "More spankings on her bottom or should I make her breasts red?"

There were different opinions from unknown voices, and I cringed.

"The decision is not unanimous," Brittney declared. "I shall have to do both."

I shook my head, pleading for mercy.

"Beg me to punish your tits, slave," Brittney said as she grabbed my chin forcefully like a mother would when scolding a child.

"Please..."

"Louder, the men can't hear you, and keep your head up."

I tried to lick my dry lips and speak around the chain. "Please...punish my tits."

"You heard her guys. She wants these delicious boobs spanked for your pleasure. Only a truly submissive woman would ever desire to endure such pain. Let's test her endurance, shall we?"

I cringed and waited for the first strike. My breasts had always been a very sensitive part of my body. I didn't know what to expect, but I knew it would hurt. All I could do was tense my body in anticipation.

I didn't have to wait long. A loud snap filled the air as a searing pain shot through the underside of my soft breasts. I cried loudly and writhed in agony for a few moments until the stinging subsided. She was using a riding crop. Another strike connected hard. I had never felt such pain before. She was hitting the most sensitive undersides of my breasts. Another strike followed by three quicker ones had me begging for mercy in short order.

"She asks for mercy!" Brittney declared.

I heard men jeering and applauding. What sort of man enjoyed watching a woman having her bare breasts flogged?

"Shall we give her mercy?" Brittney asked.

There was a unanimous no from the men watching. My heart sank. Brittney removed the chain from between my teeth and quickly removed the painful nipple clamps. I wanted to beg Brittney to be gentle, but she was already gone. I hung my head, feeling my sore breasts radiate pain as I waited.

A sudden whack from a paddle across my breast made me cry out in pain. It felt like the same paddle she used on my bottom, only now the flat surface hit my entire breast. She struck again on my other breast, mashing it with the force of her blow. More pain. Over and over she hit my tits, alternating from one to the other or giving one two or three hits and then pausing.

When Brittney finally stopped, my entire chest was throbbing and bright red. I felt pain like every pore of my skin had been stabbed with a needle. I was certain my breasts were going to turn black and blue. I heard the paddle hit the floor as she dropped it. Was my punishment over? I hoped it was.

I heard the winch again. The pressure on my wrists subsided as my arms were lowered relieving the pain in my shoulders.

Finally!

I silently thanked whoever was turning the crank for the relief they gave me. Someone, probably Brittney, unfastened the spreader bar on my ankles, and I was able to stand with a little more decency. I was still in the dark and unaware who the men around me were, or how many, but at least I wasn't strung up like a side of beef anymore. I wasn't sure how much I liked being hung from my wrists or having my bottom and breasts paddled.

"Give me your hand," Brittney said quietly. "We're done for now. You did a great job by the way. Very impressive."

"You didn't have to be so rough," I whispered, trying to keep the annoyance out of my voice. "My tits aren't used to that kind of treatment you know."

"All part of the show. Sorry, but I had to play it up."

I felt a hand take mine. Brittney led me across what I assumed was a stage and then stopped. I was still in complete darkness and wondered what was next. I could hear something heavy scraping the floor as it was moved closer to me. What it was I didn't know, but the object was placed between my legs, and I could feel the sides touching my inner calves. What the hell was going to happen next?

"Hold my hands while I help you kneel."

I nodded uncertainly and reached my hand out. With Brittney's guidance, I carefully knelt on top of whatever they had put between my legs. It felt odd and cold. In my mind I imagined I was sitting on top of one of those riding bulls you see in the funny videos; the ones where people are always falling off of.

Part of me was tempted to ask what I was sitting on, but my question died in my throat when I felt straps fastened around my lower legs and ankles pinning them to the floor. My arms were drawn back without warning which forced me to lean my torso back as well. My ass became firmly planted on whatever I was straddling. Straps suddenly bound my arms straight back leaving me unable to sit fully upright or lean forward. Finally, a thick belt was thrown over my thighs and hips and drawn tight like a seatbelt keeping my twat firmly planted. My position was uncomfortable, and I wasn't sure the purpose of it, but my questions became moot when the object I was sitting on suddenly started to vibrate.

Oh my god, a Sybian machine!

I had never been on a Sybian, but I had seen them and knew what they did. I should have guessed right away that was what I was sitting on. How stupid of me. Now I knew the reason why my legs, waist, and arms were secured. I wiggled my twat, trying to lift myself off the device but I was held firmly on top of it. Vibrations coursed through my wet pussy, stimulating every nerve fiber within it. My struggles only made the vibrations more intense. There was no escape. I was completely at the mercy of whoever held the control dial.

I gasped and moaned as unrelenting pleasure coursed through my already aroused pussy. I bucked my hips feeling my heavy breasts bounce and jiggle; the nipple clamps bit my tender nipples. I twisted my torso from side to side not caring that my breasts flopped about. No matter which way I moved the vibrations stimulated my pussy.

I wished I had control of the machine because the setting was way too high for me. The stimulation was overwhelming my senses and numbing my clit. Despite my misgivings, my mouth opened in shock as my first orgasm violently rippled through my body.

Oh, my god!

I had never cummed that fast or that hard, ever. Instead of fighting the machine, I gave in and started to grind my hips. I wanted another.

I expected that whoever was operating the Sybian would have slowed the vibrations or turned it off, after my quick orgasm but the machine kept going. My pussy was forced toward another orgasm which crested less than a minute later. It was almost painful, but I loved it.

My clit gets so sensitive after I cum and I cried in a mixture of ecstasy and pain as the vibrations continued. I begged them to slow the machine, but my words were ignored. I squeezed my pussy muscles trying to ignore the powerful ripples of another orgasm, but my third orgasm hit me even stronger. I've never had three orgasms in a row, and my body didn't know how to respond. I cried louder and started begging in earnest for mercy, but the machine kept humming.

"Please, stop! I need a rest!"

I could hear people near me making comments. A pair of hands groped my sore breasts. The vibrations from the machine continued. The more I bucked and struggled the greater my discomfort became and the greater the pleasure that followed. The best way to endure the machine might be to relax but even that only delayed the inevitable.

My fourth orgasm was so intense that my head slumped forward. I felt drained. All the pleasure I felt was replaced now with sensitive pain. A woman isn't meant to be forced to orgasm so quickly. I was certain the machine would be shut off now. There was no way they would rip five orgasms out of my body. No woman ever cummed five times in a row, did they? Was that even possible?

Instead of shutting the machine off, though, someone turned a dial, and the vibrations changed pitch to a slower deeper thrum. I cried out in pleasure. All my pain suddenly transformed into quivering sensations and I ground my hips absorbing the mechanical vibrations through my overly aroused clit. Whoever was controlling the machine knew how to extract a seemingly endless chain of orgasms from my body.

I began to beg for mercy, but none came. I panted and gasped and felt my body pull against the restraints. Another orgasm was quickly building. I had no defense against what they were doing to me and had to endure it. My pussy was hyper-aroused, and every touch rippled pleasure through me. The sensations pulsing through this industrial strength vibrate overwhelmed me. I began to grunt and beg them, whoever they were, to please turn it off. I pleaded saying I needed a break. The silence was the only reply they gave. I knew they were standing around me, strange men I didn't know, and they probably had hard cocks. That thought caused my orgasm to crest, and a shrill cry escaped my lips. My legs twitched, and my stomach contracted as my orgasm rippled and fluttered through my body. Still, the vibrations continued, but I was spent. I couldn't take another climax. Brad's name nearly escaped my throat; I was that desperate for it to end. I just needed to catch my breath. I wanted to ride the machine more, but I needed a tiny break. Please!

As if they could read my mind, someone turned the machine off. My pussy continued to tingle and hum, and I knew I had made a wet mess, but there was nothing I could do. I wanted to slump forward, but my restrained arms prevented that. I couldn't move in any direction. Helpless, I simply hung my head and tried to catch my breath. How many orgasms did I have? I lost count. I probably had as many orgasms in on the machine in five minutes that I had during my entire marriage.

Rest wasn't in the cards it appeared. I suddenly felt a hard cock pressed against my lips. Someone had straddled the Sybian knowing I couldn't move my head. I flinched at the shock of something touching my lips, and a pair of hands gripped my pigtails and tilted my head back. The cock rested across my chin and lips, the tip pressed against my nose. I could smell his musk. Maybe all the men had pulled out their cocks and were waiting in a line for blowjobs now? I wished my blindfold was gone so I could at least see the man who was offering me his cock.

Remembering that this was an evaluation and that I didn't want to displease Brad, I opened my mouth. The cock slipped between my lips. It was salty and oozing precum, but I dared not complain as I started sucking. Not knowing who I was servicing made me feel dirty and thrilled at the same time. The man could be twenty, or he could be fifty. My imagination tried to picture what he might look like based solely on the size and feel of his cock in my mouth. I knew it wasn't Brad's cock; I had sucked him off enough times to know every curve and texture of his glorious rod. The cock in my mouth, though, was a complete stranger, and despite having had so many orgasms in a row, my pussy tingled with arousal.

Was I supposed to suck him off until he came? I guessed the question was mute considering how tightly bound I was. I obviously had no choice in the matter. He would let me suck him to orgasm, or he would pull out. The decision was his. My job was just to give pleasure with my mouth.

He didn't cum, but his cock did spit up a lot. Precum was the worst part of blowjobs, in my opinion, which is why never liked sucking my husband off. I had no option to spit, so I simply forced the clear liquid down my throat. Abruptly the cock was taken out of my mouth, and I stopped. There was no thank you or appreciation of any kind. He just pulled it out of my mouth, and that was that. Was this an evaluation of my performance? Did he like it? Did I pass?

Another cock replaced it. I guessed they were all going to take turns. This new cock was fatter that the last one and I had to stretch my jaw to accommodate him. No sooner had I started a rhythm than the man stepped back and a new cock was placed in my mouth. On and on this went until I lost count of how many cocks I had sucked. I had thought to keep track of the number so I would have a rough estimate of the group in the room but soon some of the men had returned for seconds, and I cursed myself for losing track. Cock after cock slipped into my mouth and I sucked each and every one of them as best I could. Some men stayed longer than others, but thankfully none of the men had an orgasm and made me swallow.

It hadn't occurred to me at the time to ask why none of them were having orgasms. Eventually, the group blowjobs came to an end. No one told me, though, and I waited patiently with my mouth open until it became obvious there were no more cocks to suck. I tentatively closed my mouth and waited. Saliva was everywhere, and it hung off my face and chin. My aching jaw and tongue were able to rest, though, and I knew I was out of practice. I forced all the spit and precum out of my mouth and let it dribble down my chin adding to what was already there. I could feel it slide off my chin and onto my chest. I hoped no one scolded me for being so messy.

Thankfully no one turned the Sybian on again. I remained in darkness, still bound with my arms pulled back and bound while waiting and wondering what was in store for me next. No one seemed concerned about me. I was just an object to be used. I felt like a dirty spent whore, and a thrill ran up my spine. Here I was, a school teacher and married mother, strapped to a Sybian in the basement of a strip club forced to suck off men I couldn't even see. You don't get much dirtier than that, I thought. Despite my sore shoulders and being kept in complete darkness, I was enjoying my fantasy. I hoped Brad was too.

I guessed the men were taking breaks now. Eventually, after a long wait, Brittney knelt beside me. I could smell her perfume.

"You're doing well."

I smiled. "Thanks, I guess. I've never experienced anything like this."

"Are you enjoying yourself?"

I pondered the question and then nodded. "This is a Sybian machine I'm straddling?"

"Yes," Brittney replied quietly. "I enjoyed watching you thrashing around on it. Was is pleasant?"

I stifled a laugh so that I wouldn't draw attention. "Very intense. Yes, I liked it. I know part of me should be offended that complete strangers made me suck their dicks, but even that was thrilling. The loss of control while having my choices taken away gets me so horny for some reason. I need some water, please."

"Let me undo these restraints. They said you could have a five-minute break to have a stretch and a drink. Would you like something stronger than water? We have hard liquor or wine if you wish."

"No, just water. Am I done? Have I passed? When can I have this blindfold taken off so I can see my audience?"

"They are resting. There is one final session before the men vote. I think most of the guys are inclined to accept you, but some appear to be on the fence. Your Dom is arguing on your behalf. You are a very lucky submissive."

Was I? Was Brad pleading my case? Was I that bad that he needed to argue on my behalf? I nodded, not wishing to expose any ignorance of the dominant and submissive roles. I was still learning what this lifestyle was about, and though I understood a lot, it was becoming clear that I still had more to learn. Even though I thought I performed well, from Brittney's comments, it seemed I didn't please all the men. My heart sank. My thoughts drifted to my husband and son. I wondered what he would think if he knew I had pleasured so many men with my mouth. I wondered too what my school principle would think if he discovered one of his teachers was a slut-slave. That last thought made me cringe. I would be fired instantly if my boss found out.

As Brittney removed the restraints, I rubbed my shoulders and aching wrists. She helped me stand, and I found my legs unstable and weak.

"So I have to keep this blindfold on?"

"I'm afraid so. Once the evaluation is over, someone will remove it, and you can finally see the men you pleasured. The men in this club will all become your dominant in a way, and you will be required to be submissive to each and every one just as I am."

I didn't know what to say, so I remained quiet. What did Brittney mean I would have to be submissive to each and every member of the bondage club? Brittney led me off the stage and parted a thick curtain which I could feel as I stepped through.

"Hold still, we're alone now."

I didn't move. Brittney lifted my blindfold and gently peeled the medical tape off my eyelids. I felt a little confused. With the tape gone, I opened my eyes and blinked at the sharp brightness of everything.

"I thought I had to keep that on?"

"I was instructed to give you a break. I can apply fresh tape and blindfold once your break is over. I just thought it would be more comfortable if you had a moment to feel normal."

What was normal? I was in the basement of a strip-club being used sexually by men I didn't know or could even see. I examined my torn school girl outfit in dismay, holding the tattered fabric in my hands. I liked the outfit and wished whoever had torn it would have instead just asked me to remove it. I pulled it over my head and crumpled the ruined costume into a ball. I was still wearing the high heels and my white stockings, but with the costume gone, I suddenly felt more vulnerable.

Brittney handed me a bottle of water. I tore the cap off and drank it down, washing the salty aftertaste of so many sweaty cocks from my mouth. She glanced at her watch but said nothing. I took the moment of respite to stretch my tender shoulders and rub my chaffed wrists. I hoped my husband didn't ask about the marks on my skin. I would have to concoct a believable excuse, but none came to mind just yet.

"Can you tell me what my next session will be?"

Brittney only smiled.

"Come on, none of the men are listening. Just a little hint?"

"Are you on a birth control pill?"

Her question startled me. "Why?"

Brittney walked to the curtain and made a tiny slit before peering out. A moment later, she came back and looked me in the eyes. "They're probably all going to have sex with you."

I blinked in dismay. "All of the men out there?"

She nodded. "They had sex with me during my trials. They do it with all new submissives. Every man. They do it so when a new Dominant joins the club with his Submissive; there is no jealousy or envy. Each man has already had access to the girl, and because she knows they have all used her, there is less resistance to being sampled again. I hope they let you join. In the future, you're going to love bondage parties, especially the orgies."

"Orgies?" I asked in shock. I didn't know what to think of the idea. In my heart, I was content with simply being Brad's submissive. The idea that strangers will be having intercourse with me, though? Sure it was a fantasy, but to turn that fantasy into reality? I felt uneasy. I wasn't sure I was ready to try group sex, especially with unknown men. Were they all tested for disease? I wasn't on the pill either. Sex with so many men infinitely increased my risk of becoming pregnant.

Did I even want strangers fucking me? If they were handsome men, then possibly. But what if half the men on the other side of the curtain were fat hairy pasty men? I wasn't going to risk pregnancy so a large sweaty man could have his jollies. Part of me was excited, and the other part horrified. I thought of Brad. He would be humiliated if I backed out now. I felt a tinge of unfairness, though. No one had bothered to ask me if this was something I wanted to do. Just the courtesy of asking would have been nice. I would have agreed, but it wasn't fair bringing a new submissive like me into a situation like this without at least talking about it. Brad knew my position on risking pregnancy.

"Have you ever had anal sex?" Brittney asked.

My eyes grew wide as I looked at her. "No, never! Am I expected to?"

Brittney nodded gravely. "Oh dear. I'm not sure they know you're an anal virgin. I should speak to your Dom right away and let him know."

"He already knows," I said quickly. "I'm going to have strangers force their cocks up my bum? I've never done that, and frankly, the idea scares me a little."

"Hold on a moment," Brittney said as she held up a hand. "Let me think what the protocols are in a situation like this. Frankly, I'm startled your Dom would even put you in a situation like this. I just assumed you were well seasoned."

"Well, I'm not. I'm just a housewife having an affair," I blurted before I could clamp my mouth shut. I hadn't meant to reveal the last part. I stared at Brittney, my heart beating like a war drum in my chest.

"You're certain your Dom knows you never had anal before?"

"Yes, Brad and I talked about it just a few days ago. And he knows I'm not on the pill and can't risk pregnancy!"

"Because of your husband? I understand. I didn't think there were many women your age who were still anal virgins."

"Gee, thanks. Not everyone has tried it," I said dryly.

"Okay, because this hasn't happened before, I'll risk mentioning it. In the meantime, take this butt plug and lube, and work it in there. You need to be well lubricated and stretched. Otherwise, the pain will be too much."

I watched as Brittney walked to a red and black colored storage trunk. She opened the lid and rummaged through various sealed Tupperware containers until finding the one she was looking for. She peeled the top off the container and grabbed a crinkly package from inside. She handed the package to me with a smile. Inside was pink tapered butt plug and a tube of lubricant. She then walked to the thick curtain before looking back at me.

"Open the package, Julie, and put the plug in. I'll see what I can do about all of this. Be right back."

I nodded dumbly and peered at the butt plug. I'd seen plugs on the internet and even watched videos of girls putting them up their butts. For some reason, I couldn't get my hands to move, though. I knew I should lubricate my anus and the plug, but I continued to stare at it in disbelief. Was I about lose something I was saving for a special occasion with Brad? My first experience with anal was going to be group sex? My hand was trembling. Could I do this? I didn't think I could. This was too big a step. Brad should have known what I was comfortable with trying, and what was beyond my hard limits.

For the first time, since Brad and I had become intimate, I had serious doubts in my mind. Anal sex was too personal for me to share with strangers. Vaginal sex risked pregnancy. Any one of those men could get me pregnant. What would I tell my husband?

I felt a stab of anger. I was in this situation because Brad decided not to consult with me first. If he had, I would have pointed out I'm not on the pill, and I wasn't wild about a group of men I didn't know putting their cocks up my butt.

The curtains parted, and I looked up. Brad strode in with Brittney close behind. He glanced at what I was holding and then folded his arms. He looked like he was annoyed that I was wasting his time. I couldn't care less.

"You want me to have anal sex?" I asked, standing to face him. "With total strangers?"

He raised an eyebrow and glanced over his shoulder at Brittney. She just shrugged, preferring to leave the decision in his hands. He turned his eyes back towards me, and I dreaded his answer.

"I thought you loved me."

His words struck me square in the chest. "I do love you, sweaty."

"I went through a lot of trouble arranging this and convincing these men that you were quality material. Maybe I was mistaken," Brad said quietly.

"What are you saying?"

"I thought we had something special, something not a lot of people ever experience together. I was opening up new horizons for you. Are you not my submissive pet?"

I swallowed hard. "Yes, yes, of course, my love. I'm all that. It's just that I'm nervous, sweetheart. I've never had anal sex. That's all. Everything else has been great, honest. I'm just a little scared."

Brad frowned and shook his head. "I'm disappointed in you, thinking about yourself instead of those men out there. If you want, we can leave, but if we do leave, then I'm going to have to reevaluate our relationship. I thought I was grooming an eager submissive woman. Perhaps I was wrong."

I dropped to my knees and pleaded. "Please, no. I'll be good. Forgive me, Master for being so silly. I will do whatever you want. Please, just don't leave me. I need you. I want you."

He seemed unconvinced.

"I'll do it. I'll let your friends do what they want with me. You'll see, I can be obedient. Forgive me for being afraid. I trust you."

"Well," Brad said stroking his chin. "I believe you. Perhaps I've pushed you a little too hard, and because you've agreed to submit, I will speak to the emcee and inquire about changing the routine. If I do this for you, Julie, you had better show me proper gratefulness later."

I hugged his leg and planted kisses on his shoes. "Thank you, Master. I will do whatever you wish. I'm yours. Please, I'm just not ready yet, but I will obey."

"Let me see what I can arrange. Can I expect you to complain again?"

"No, Master. The slave will obey. I love you."

"Very well, stay here," Brad said and turned on his heel. He paused and cupped Brittney's breasts briefly before leaning in for a kiss.

My eyes bulged, and a stab of jealousy flared through my soul as I watched Brad and Brittney kiss each other. I clamped my mouth shut and looked away. How dare she kiss my man? Had he fucked her before?

When Brad left, I waited until the curtain stopped moving before turning my eyes towards Brittney. "Do you like kissin my Master?"

She grinned. "Very much. Is that jealousy I detect?"

"Maybe."

"You should let that go around here. You forget that I'm a submissive just like you. If a man wants to kiss and fondle me, I cannot refuse."

I felt a little mollified. Brittney handed another bottle of water to me.

My five-minute break turned into a lot more. I hoped my qualms about having anal sex weren't ruining our chances of joining the bondage club. I chastised myself for caving into Brad so quickly. I had seen a side of Brad, though, that I had never witnessed before. He could be charming and sweet on one hand, and domineering and almost cruel on the other. I drank from my water bottle and waited. My legs were humming with nervous energy and wouldn't stop bouncing.

Brittney sat beside me and placed her arm around my shoulders. I could do nothing but wait while I wondered what the men on the other side of that curtain would decide to do with my body. I leaned into Brittney and felt a tear roll down my cheek.

When Brad returned, his face was unreadable as he looked at me.

"What have you decided, Master?" I asked weakly, brushing a tear away.

He was silent for a moment and then pointed to the pink buttplug in my hands. "Put that in, Julie. Brittney, get the tape and blindfold on her. I want you two out here in five minutes. You've disappointed me, slut."

I cringed as my face contorted in anguish. I reached for Brad, but he brushed my hand away, turned and parted the curtains as he left. *No. Please god, no!*

"Looks like you're doing group anal," Brittney said quietly.

I bit my lip and started to cry.

While sitting behind the red velvet curtain in the cold basement of the strip club, I shivered as I stared in dismay at the retreating figure of the man I thought I loved. Brittney dried my tears which flowed after Brad so dismissively brushed my fears aside. He knew I was nervous about trying anal sex, so why was he asking me to let strangers do that very thing to me? I felt like I was just a whore in his eyes and not a woman roleplaying a submissive. Did Brad really think my only purpose in life was to pleasure men? Those men had no regard for my feelings, they just wanted a submissive woman willing to take it the ass. All they wanted was as a woman to satisfy their cocks, and that woman was me.

Brittney had a concerned expression on her face as she folded the tissue in her hand and dabbed my cheek again. "Do you want to invoke your safe word, Julie?"

I knew she had gone through a similar initiation when she joined the bondage club. I could take her advice and use my safe word and bring the session to a stop. It would be that easy. The submissive had all the power and the final say in how she was treated. But I didn't want to use my safe word. Part of me wanted to try anal sex. I just wasn't comfortable with the setting, or the fact that I didn't know any of the men, or the fact that all of this was just dumped on me without warning. I just needed some time to warm up to the idea of an anal gangbang and I didn't think my reticent stance was too outrageous. Brad should not have brushed aside my concerns so callously.

If debasing myself meant that much to Brad, then I would do for him. I wanted Brad to see my tears and know the damage he was doing to our relationship. Part of me hoped he would understand that some fantasies are better left to the imagination. Maybe using my safe word was a good idea after all. No. I'll play the dirty whore and let Brad see my heart wither from the disrespect he was showing me.

"Thank you, but no," I said, sounding braver than I felt. "I'm going to see this through." An overwhelming sense of helplessness washed over me. I was committed.

"You're certain?"

I nodded and then sniffled. Brittney dabbed my cheek again. *I can do this.*

"Do you want to insert the anal plug yourself, or do you want me to?" Brittney asked. Her expression changed to one of pity.

I suppressed a shudder and looked at the tapered pink plug in her hand. Picking the tube of lubricant off the table, I flipped the top and sniffed the contents. There was no odor. I pinched a drop between my fingers and rubbed them together. The lubricant was slippery and clear.

"This is so humiliating," I said quietly. "I don't know if I can do it."

Brittney nodded. "I can turn away if you'd like and give you privacy."

"Maybe that would help, thank you."

When Brittney had swiveled her back toward me, I squeezed lubricant onto my fingers and then tentatively rubbed them around the rim of my anus. The liquid was cool. I shuddered in disgust and greased as best I could. Then with more lubricant, I slipped my fingers into my butthole and worked them around in small circles. It felt degrading, but it was the only way to lessen the coming pain. My hole was way too tight to be penetrated by fingers, let alone hard cocks. I didn't know how girls in porn videos did it. I applied more to my fingers and tried to force as much into my butthole as I could. After a while, it felt slippery and wet, but I wasn't content. I squeezed more lube once again and tried my best to force it in. You could never have too much lube for anal, I thought. Next, I poured lubricant around the surface of the butt plug and rubbed it all over making sure there wasn't a dry spot left. Now for the really humiliating part, I thought.

I brought the plug between my legs and pressed the tip against my unwilling rosebud. My hole tightened in protest, and I had to relax my sphincter slightly. Finally, just a little of the plug slipped in. I waited and held my breath and then worked the plug back and forth until I had enough courage to insert it further. Sucking in my breath, I pushed the plug deeper and felt my butthole cry in protest as it was stretched and forced open. The painful feeling was unnatural, but the lubricant helped. I winced as my sphincter slipped around the widest point and then closed around the tapered base. I felt strange. Never in my life had anything been pushed into my ass and yet here I was, sitting in the cold basement of a strip club forcing a butt plug in. The constant pressure inside my bum reminded me of what was to come. If a small plug was this uncomfortable, then what would a thick ramming cock feel like penetrating me? Could I even do this? I wanted to experience anal sex; then this was going to be a serious first time. I just hoped I was up for it.

"I'm done putting it in," I said quietly. My cheeks felt bright red.

Brittney spun around and looked at me. "Are you okay?"

"It feels weird, but I'm okay," I said with a nod. It was a lie. It felt more than weird. It felt violating, but I wanted to put on a brave face, so I smiled too.

"Okay, then close your eyes. I'll apply the tape again. Be strong, Julie."

"Thanks," I whispered and shut my eyes.

I heard Brittney pull three strips of medical tape off the roll. She placed them over my left eye, sealing it shut and then repeated the process for my right. I didn't need a blindfold, but I figured it was probably meant to cover the unsightly look of a woman with her eyes taped shut. When Brittney finished applying the blindfold, I reached out with my hand, and she gripped it. In complete darkness, I stood. My stomach was fluttering, and my knees felt weak.

"How do I look?" I asked nervously. I still wore the stiletto heels and white crotchless stockings, but nothing else except the butt plug.

"You have a great body, Julie. I'm afraid those men are going to love it."

"A submissive slave obeys men who want to use her. Isn't that the rule?"

Brittney didn't reply.

"Lead me out there. Let's get this over with," I said. I just hoped my virgin ass had enough lubricant in it to make Brad happy.

I felt Brittney's gentle hand guide me through the curtains and back onto the stage. My stiletto heels clicked with each uncertain step I took. My ass felt wet and slippery, and the plug was uncomfortable, but it stayed in. Brittney stopped and released my hand. I heard a whisper of encouragement, but I ignored it. I held my chin up, trying to maintain my dignity while I stood patiently. I knew the eyes of every man was probably feasting on my naked body with anticipation. Let them stare, I thought. I wasn't doing this for them.

Brad whispered quietly into my ear, "Is it in?"

I nodded robotically. "Yes, Master."

"Good. Turn around and bend over. Show them the plug."

I felt my flush deepen. Brad's arm turned me in a half circle, and I leaned forward. Resting my hands on my knees, I arched my back thrusting my ass out. I felt my cheeks part and knew my butt plug was in full view. I was beyond mortified but knew I had to get used to such feelings if I was to join the bondage club.

147

Is this what you want? Is this what all men want? A virgin butthole to plunge their cocks into? Well here, take mine. Make me cry in pain.

Brad's hand was on my arm again. I followed his lead, stepping carefully, my bare breasts swaying as I walked. He moved his hands to my shoulders and walked me for a distance. Then he spun me to my left, until, with the slightest of pressure on my shoulders, he stopped my turn. I had no idea where I was on the stage or in what direction I was facing. The cool air made my nipples stand erect, and I shivered.

"Sit down," Brad said. He gave me his arm for support as I bent my knees. In my mind, there was nothing but darkness under me. I had to trust I would soon find a perch to sit on, and I did. It was something cold and hard.

"Lean back. You're on a small table," Brad whispered.

He supported my arms as I leaned backward and then cradled my head as it touched the table. So I would be on my back, I thought. The men probably wanted to see the pain on my face as they penetrated my ass or be free to grope my breasts or both perhaps.

"Brad, I'm scared," I whispered. My body was trembling.

His hand caressed the side of my face, and I fought the urge to sob suddenly.

"You can do this. Remember this is your fantasy."

Not anal! His words didn't comfort me at all. I then felt rope bite into my ankles as Brad began to bind me. Once both of my ankles were secured, I felt my legs lifted and spread apart, exposing my privates and making them easily accessible. Why did I have to be blindfolded and tied? The darkness made my fears spike. I hated being so vulnerable while not knowing how many men were in the room or what they looked like. All I knew was what they would do to me.

Brad then fastened a thick belt over my pelvis securing my ass in place over the edge of the table. He pulled the ropes around my ankles further apart until they formed a wide 'V' and then tied them to something. I was spread wide and unable to move which made me feel even more vulnerable and exposed.

Someone placed each of my hands on what felt like handle bars embedded in the table top. I gripped each bar obediently and then felt restraints placed around my wrists. I guessed the bars were there for me to hold onto so I didn't slide off the table while being fucked. My stomach knotted, and I couldn't stop trembling.

Another strap was placed just below my bare breasts and secured tightly while yet another went around my neck. How many restraints did I need to have on me? A sudden hand grabbed my breast, and I flinched. There was nothing I could do to prevent the hand groping me, so I endured it. Then a finger slipped into my pussy rather roughly. I didn't know if it was the same man groping my tits or someone else entirely. I clamped my mouth shut and endured the humiliation. I was nothing more than a helpless doll strapped to a table.

When I felt my butt plug suddenly pushed back and forth, I yelped. A hand quickly covered my mouth and pinched my nostrils shut. I felt my heart start to race as my airflow was cut off. The plug in my ass was pulled out to the widest point and then pushed back in roughly. I struggled, but the hand over my mouth and nose pressed even harder. I fought the urge to panic and tensed my body against the pushing and pulling of my butt plug. *Please let me breathe!*

"Gentlemen, please gather around the table here," Brad said.

I heard movement. The hand covering my nose and mouth disappeared and I sucked in as much air as I could. Brad was gathering the entire group of men to stand around my naked body. Thankfully whoever was playing with my butt plug had also stopped. I was helpless, though, with my legs spread wide and my body strapped to the table. I tightened my grip on the bracing bars and waited. This wasn't the way I had envisioned having my first anal sex. My way was far more romantic and included flowers and candles and soft music, not being bound on my back to a table and blindfolded while strangers stood watching.

"I would like to introduce to you, my submissive slut-slave, Julie. I've been grooming her to be my fuck toy since early September of last year, and as you can see, she has made tremendous progress in her submission," Brad said.

I imagined eyes looking all over my body, and I cringed. He spoke as if I wasn't a person and it hurt my feelings, but I also knew this was part of role-playing, so maybe he didn't mean what he said. Even so, his words did raise questions in my mind. Was his plan the entire time to turn me his little fuck toy? I didn't believe it. Even though I was married, Brad and I had made a connection. We were practically soul mates married to separate people. I wasn't anybody's fuck toy and dismissed his words as role-playing despite how much they stung.

"Julie is a school teacher. She might even have taught some of your kids. The important thing to remember is that this twenty-four-year-old hottie has only had sex with her husband, and even then, hardly ever. Today, we're going to change that."

There were murmurs and quiet laughter. I strained against the bindings. Why did Brad have to demean me like that verbally? Wasn't it enough that I was bound and tied to a table and willing to play out his fantasy?

"As you can see, Julie's body is flawless. For a young mother, you'd expect flabby tits and a sagging ass, but she is firm and tone. I'd like to point out how adorable her little orgasms are and how her body trembles when she cums. I've been able to dominate her submissive personality and train her to suck cock and even swallow. Despite her young age, she is thoroughly broken in and tamed for use. Trust me, she will do whatever you want."

More laughter and guffaws. I fought the urge to defend my dignity. Each of the words Brad spoke hurt me more and more. Did Brad think of me as some sexual conquest? It couldn't be true.

"I would like for us to be accepted into this bondage club, and I hope her performance today will earn your votes. If not, then I think her next special performance will convince those of you still sitting on the fence," Brad said.

There was more laughter.

Brad waited for the laughter to fade to silence. Then, in a serious tone that demanded respect, he said, "Julie is an anal virgin."

The men gasped and I felt my face burn with humiliation.

"In a few moments, I will fuck her virgin ass for your viewing pleasure. Do not be concerned with what she thinks or feels or how much she cries, she has given her consent, and she knows her purpose in life is to pleasure men. Now, I want you all to stand closer and watch this special event. Feel free to touch her body."

The men around me cheered and clapped. I desperately wanted my blindfold taken off at that moment. I wanted to see the faces of these men who would cheer while my ass was penetrated for their amusement. I also wanted to look Brad in the eyes and see if there was truth to his words. Did he view me as a *fuck toy*?

My thoughts vanished from my mind the moment I felt my butt plug being pulled out. I winced and gripped the table handles harder as my body tensed. This was it, I thought, I was about to have anal sex for the first time in my life. My breathing quickened as I fought the urge to cry. I had to be brave, I told myself. I suddenly wished there wasn't an audience watching.

"Julie, beg me to fuck your tight little ass," Brad said to me.

What? He wanted me to beg for my humiliation? I was more than willing to try anal sex with him, but not like this. I wanted it to be a special occasion and in private. Anal was the one thing my husband wanted that I still denied him, and the one thing I could give Brad that was special. Did he want to cheapen my gift by making me beg for anal sex in front of strangers?

"Beg!" Brad shouted.

I felt the sting of a crop against my breast and winced. He struck again hitting the soft underside of my breast. Pain radiated through my chest, and I gasped.

"Please!" I cried. The room fell silent as every ear waited. I took a few breaths and settled my nerves. "Please, Master..."

His crop struck again, and I thrashed against my bonds in frustration. Why did he have to hit my sensitive breasts?

"Your Master desires it, slave. Beg me to do it."

I relented and turned my head towards the sound of his voice. If I didn't give Brad my permission, then I knew he would force himself on me anyway. I had given him permission. Perhaps making me beg was part of the theatrics, designed to impress the men watching. Maybe Brad wanted to show that he had control over his pet?

"Please, put it in my ass," I heard my voice say. "I want it."

153

There was applause, and I felt my heart break. Brad must have felt triumphant. I couldn't see his, or anyone else's face, but I could imagine the lustful glee they must be showing. In the darkness of my blindfold, I waited for his cock to enter my butt.

The butt plug had loosened my anus, but it still didn't prepare me for the pain of Brad's thick cock as it pressed against me. I grunted and squeezed the hand holds until my knuckles felt like breaking. The pressure felt unnatural as he worked the tip of his cock into my reluctant hole. I couldn't tell how far in he had gone, but I knew he was in. I just focused on ignoring the comments and jeers of the men around me as a tear, that escaped my taped eyes, rolled down my cheek and into my hair.

"You see, gentlemen. The trick to fucking any woman up the ass is stretching her unwilling hole, but not too much. You still want to have pleasure," Brad said as if he was an expert on the subject. Maybe he was. There were guffaws all around me as I imagined men leaning closer to watch.

"It hurts," I whimpered. "Be gentle, please."

"No one gives a fuck what you think," Brad said in a degrading tone. I felt my pain increase as he thrust an angry cock into me as if to prove his point. He grabbed my spread legs roughly and started to ram his cock in and out of my asshole without regard for my pain.

I cried and whimpered. It felt like Brad's cock was splitting my ass open. I thrashed against the bindings, but my body couldn't move. My stomach clenched, and I tensed my legs, trying to pry my ass away so the pain would subside, but there was nothing I could do. The discomfort was overwhelming.

"Do you like it?" Brad asked.

"Yes, Master," I lied. In truth, it was almost as painful as giving birth.

What had I gotten myself into? Why was I having anal sex in front of an audience? Did I have no shame? I was doing this for Brad, but he seemed so aggressive about it.

Brad paused his fucking. Perhaps he was tired, or too close to orgasm and needed a break. I welcomed to relief it gave my stretched hole.

"Beg me to continue," Brad said after a moment.

Hadn't I already given him permission to try anal? Now he wanted to rub my nose in humiliation? Fine. I could play the submissive slave girl for him.

"Please, fuck me harder. Don't stop, Master!" I said loud enough for everyone to hear. If I was going to lose my anal virginity like this, then I might as well try to impress the audience with my willingness. I didn't want them to think I was weak or that I was broken.

Brad sank further into me and then pulled out and pushed in again with slow, steady movements. I felt my hole stretched to accommodate him, but the pain didn't lessen much. Finally, he sank the entire length of his cock into me, and I felt his hips touch the back of my ass cheeks. My ass throbbed, but the pain did subside a little, which surprised me. Perhaps I was getting used to his girth at last.

"To think, ten months ago she was a naive school teacher in an unhappy marriage," Brad said to the men around him, his cock still buried to the hilt in my ass. "Now she is strapped to a table begging for anal. You see what you can achieve when you put your mind to it? I own her. And now, I'm going to pump her sweet little ass until I cum."

I felt his grip around my legs tighten as he withdrew his cock. I don't know how far he pulled out, but from the pressure, I guessed he left the head still inside of me. He then rammed it home, and I cried out in pain. He didn't stop once he had sunk to the hilt the second time. Instead, he withdrew and thrust himself into me again a little faster. I bit my lip and braced my body. He slammed into me again and again, each time harder and faster than before. My ass screamed in pain. There wasn't enough lubricant, but Brad didn't care. He humped me furiously, his grunts filling the air with grotesque lust. This was something he had been dreaming about doing for months, and nothing was going to stop him now it seemed. My body rocked with each hump he made, but the bindings held me in place. I could feel my bare breasts jiggle and bounce each time his hips slammed into my ass cheeks.

For some reason I couldn't fathom, my pussy tingled with arousal. What the hell? Was I getting aroused now? Was it the thought of mysterious men watching me that got me hot? Maybe I was starting to enjoy anal sex, and it was a mixture of pleasure and pain. Sensations I never experienced before coursed through my abdomen. The initial pain of being penetrated had subsided. My hole felt stretched and relaxed enough to accommodate his cock more comfortably. It was still painful, but I was able to loosen my grip on the table bars. Part of me was finally starting to enjoy the feeling of anal sex, and it surprised me.

"Please, Master," I begged. "I need to cum."

My words must have startled Brad because he stopped fucking my ass. There was movement, and I took the respite to catch my breath and settle my fluttering heart. I suddenly felt something cold and hard pressed against my clit. A moment later a low thrumming vibration pulsated through my pussy. I gasped and cried in pleasure. Brad resumed his relentless humping. With each thrust into my butt, my pussy inched closer to orgasm from the vibrator pressed against my clit. I had never experienced such pleasure in my life, and suddenly, I wanted more.

"Fuck me harder, Master. Please, harder!" I begged. Some men cheered, but I ignored them all. I just wanted Brad to give me an orgasm. What started as an unpleasant experience was turning into a gigantic thrill I had never experienced before.

Brad continued slamming his cock in and out of my ass, and I knew I couldn't take it much longer. Sensations were flooding through my body. My legs began to tremble, and my stomach was clenching. I was about to have a huge, mind-blowing orgasm and there was nothing I could do to stop it.

"Permission to cum, Master!" I cried in desperation; my voice sounded three octaves too high.

"No, not yet," Brad said, his reply labored. He kept humping me, this cock sliding in and out of my anus like a steady jackhammer. He had to be close to an orgasm by now.

"Please! I can't hold on!" I begged. A mixture of pleasure and pain washed over me. It was incredible!

Rough hands grabbed my breasts, but I didn't care. My nipples were pulled and squeezed by someone and the pain only added to my cresting orgasm. I began to whimper. All my focus was on clenching and denying my orgasm until given permission to cum. I knew it was important for a woman not to orgasm without permission, and I didn't want to disappoint Brad. I clenched my pussy muscles and held on as best I could, but I knew it was a losing battle. My ass pounding was relentless, each thrust coursing pleasure through my body amplified by the vibrator on my clit. For god's sake how much longer was he going to take?

"Please!?"

"Not yet," Brad said, his cock pounding my ass without slowing.

My breasts were groped and by another pair of rough hands. I felt my orgasm getting closer despite my efforts to delay it. I cried out in a mixture of pain and pleasure, holding it back with the barest of threads.

"Okay slut, now!" Brad said as he reached his orgasm. His cock exploded inside my ass as he drove it home. He grunted as each spurt of cum erupted from his cock. I loved the sound of Brad's orgasms. They were so primal.

I trembled and let go of my muscles as an orgasm rocked my body. I convulsed and gasped as my legs twitched. I thrashed against the bindings. Hands released my breasts, and I tried to arch my back, but the straps held me to the table. I pulled against the bindings, flexing my muscles. My violent orgasm erupted, and my pussy started to squirt. I had never squirted in my life, but I lost all muscle control and couldn't help it. The vibrator held against my clit continued sending waves of pleasure crashing over my body to the point where it began to hurt. I couldn't take the vibrator anymore.

"Please stop! No more!" I begged. To my relief, the vibrator was removed from my clit, and Brad pulled his spent cock out of my butt. I was given a few minutes to recuperate as my body continued to tremble and convulse. My mind felt blank. I had never cummed so hard in my entire life, and it left me exhausted and humiliated that I squirted in front of total strangers. If that was anal sex, then I wanted more.

"Gentlemen, how was that?" Brad asked.

I heard applause and admiration from every direction, but I didn't care. I felt spent, lost in an ocean of warm pleasure and those men could do whatever they wanted to me for all I cared. I had just experienced the most intense orgasm of my life, and all I wanted was a few minutes to savor the experience.

"Slut," I heard Brad's voice addressing me. "Did you enjoy that?"

To be honest, I had and nodded my head. "Yes, Master. Thank you."

"You see, all a woman needs is a strong man to guide her. She enjoyed it. She thought she wouldn't, but she did. And she will enjoy it in her ass again with each of you, but not today my friends."

What did he mean not today? I felt completely submissive. The mysterious men around me could have my body. I was content and willing. Brad had broken me. If they gave me a little break, and more lubricant, I was certain, I could handle one or two more men having a go in my ass.

"I would ask that you not to penetrate her ass today. I gave her a pretty good fucking, and she needs some time to recover. I know many of you want to, but she will need time. Instead, I offer you her fertile pussy."

My mind snapped back to the present. Did Brad just offer my exposed pussy to these men instead of my butthole? I tried to lift my head, but the strap around my throat prevented it.

"Brad, no. Not that," I hissed.

"Slut Brittney, remove her blindfold and let her see the men about to use her."

I felt my blindfold yanked off and then Brittney's fingers gently peeling the tape from my eyelids. Once the tape was gone, I opened my eyes. Brad was standing between my spread legs. He looked at me and smiled. I looked at him questioningly, but he turned away.

"Remove the strap around her neck and prop her up," Brad ordered. "I want Julie to watch as her pussy is fucked helplessly."

Brittney first loosened and then removed my throat strap. I glanced at her face, and she offered me a gentle smile. "You did great. How was it?" she whispered.

"It hurt at first. I need to talk to Brad and can you bring me some water?"

Brittney shook her head, and I felt my spirits dashed. Someone propped the end of my table up. I could see the table I was strapped to was hinged. I was in a reclined position staring down my body at my bound and spread legs. I had better not get pregnant; I thought while trying to get Brad's attention.

Now that I could see I looked at the men in the room. A quick count told me there were nine of them, ten if I included Brad. To my utter amazement, I saw that there were also nine women in the room. I made number ten. They were all young and beautiful. Each man must have brought his submissive, just like Brad had brought me. I briefly wondered if each woman had gone through the same humiliating initiation as I was going through now.

"I think the emcee of today's events should have the honor of going first," Brad said. He offered me like I was nothing more than an object to be shared.

My thoughts were interrupted when a large hairy man appeared between my legs. I glanced at him and then my jaw dropped in horror as recognition filled me with shock. The man was none other than my boss, Principal Rowe.

"Hello, Julie. I've waited a long time to fuck your tight cunt."

"Principal Rowe?" I asked in shock. What the hell was he doing here? Was my boss the head of the bondage club? I would never have suspected such a thing. I shook my head to clear my eyes, but he was still there.

Rowe gestured, and I watched as a young woman appeared from the crowd. She stood beside him, and then lifted her head and looked at me.

I gasped. That was impossible! Standing naked and in complete submission to Rowe was my teaching colleague, Jennifer. She was newly hired, fresh out of teacher's college, and I often wondered how she got a job at our school so quickly. An opportunistic whore if ever there was one, Jennifer must have sucked and fucked her way into a job.

"Jennifer?" I asked, hiding my disdain for her. "What are you doing here?"

"Securing my career. I'm Mr. Rowe's special friend," Jennifer said with a smile. She snuggled against his fat hairy belly and leaned her head on his chest.

"Now I'm going to fuck you, Julie," Rowe said.

He fiddled with his cock and slipped it between my wet pussy lips. I felt a wave of revulsion course through me as I watched my principal slide his cock into me. He wasn't well endowed, but I did feel a little pleasure. I squeezed my eyes shut and waited for him to finish. It would be a mental image could never forget. My fat hairy boss was fucking me. Gross!!!

"Oh, she is tight," I heard Rowe announce to those listening. His cock made wet plunging sounds as his balls slapped against my ass cheeks. I never felt more repulsed in all my life and yet his cock gave me pleasure. Principal Rowe was the ugliest man I had ever seen naked, and I turned my head to the side and imagined he was someone else.

"Is she as tight as me?" Jennifer asked with a note of jealousy in her voice.

I opened my eyes and stared at her. She could have Rowe, I almost said. My eyes drifted to the contorted face of my principal as he concentrated on plowing me with his cock. It was an image I couldn't unsee and immediately regretted looking at him. My stomach churned. *Oh god please get it over with!* I felt a familiar tingle in my pussy, and my eyes bulged with alarm. *No way. There was no way I was going to orgasm all over his disgusting fat cock.*

"She is looser than you, my little fuck pig," Rowe said. He pulled Jennifer into his arms and cupped her perky little breast with his hairy mitten. I watched them kiss with a mix of fascination and revulsion. Why was she letting a man like that even touch her? Jennifer was a beautiful young blonde woman. She would have gotten hired as a teacher eventually. Was she that desperate for a job to hitch her wagon to him?

As I watched him fondle and kiss Jennifer, I felt my pussy start to quiver. No, I begged it. Please don't orgasm. But watching my boss and another teacher make out while he fucked me was too strange. I gasped and grunted. Mr. Rowe turned his attention towards me and started humping faster. Sweat dripped off his brow, and his fat belly developed a shine. I felt revulsion, but my pussy was too stimulated. I was beyond mortified.

Fuck it!

I gasped and gripped the table handles as my contractions came and I cummed. *Shit shit shit!* I was humiliated. Now my principal will always know he made me orgasm. I felt shame burn my cheeks as he redoubled his efforts.

"Oh, here it comes. Yeah, take my load, Julie. I've wanted to cum in you for so long. You're going to take every last drop. Beg me to cum in you!"

I bit my lip, recovering from my climax quickly.

"I said beg!" Rowe barked. Jennifer stared at me with a disapproving look. I was defying her Master, and she didn't like it.

I relented. "Please, Principal Rowe. Please cum in my *fertile* womb." I wanted him to know that I could get pregnant. Perhaps the hint would give him pause. I was wrong.

He grinned and slammed his cock home. By the convulsions of his face and the way his fat body tensed, I guessed he was spurting inside of me. I couldn't feel anything but shame as I lay with my legs spread wide. He gave me a couple of extra thrusts before sighing and pulling his spent cock from between my wet pussy lips. I could see disgusting driblets of white on the tip of his cock.

Jennifer immediately dropped to her knees and took his cock in her mouth. I cringed at the thought of sucking such a grotesque man. She slurped and sucked and licked his shaft clean. I watched as Rowe patted her on the head and then pointed towards my spread legs.

"Clean her cunt. Suck as much out as you can."

What? No! I gasped in shock. Jennifer moved her head between my legs, and I felt her mouth on my pussy before I could even protest. I wasn't into that! I had never had another woman's lips on my privates, let alone a fellow teacher's. Rowe grinned and watched as Jennifer licked and sucked.

Oh, that felt good. I bit my lip and watched her face between my legs.

"She is trained," Principal Rowe said when he noticed my eyes on her.

I shut my eyes and tried to ignore the pleasure her mouth was giving me. She sucked and sucked and cleaned my pussy with her mouth. I don't know how long it took, but when she was done, she stood and smiled at me. Her lips were glistening, and there was spent cum on her chin. A few more minutes of her mouth on me and I would have had another humiliating orgasm.

"Fetch me a drink, pet," Rowe ordered. Jennifer nodded and scurried away. He paused and looked at me. "Tell anyone, and you'll be fired."

I shook my head in shock. "I would never say a word, sir."

"Good. See that you don't. I can't wait to fuck you up the ass. Julie, you have a fine tight pussy. See you Monday."

I didn't know what to say. Mr. Rowe walked away, and I was alone for a moment. There was no indication how long I would remain strapped on my back, but from the hungry looks of the other men in the room, I knew I wouldn't be alone for long.

A few minutes later another man appeared between my legs. He grabbed my breasts and jiggled them like toys, ignoring my glare. I didn't recognize him, which was good. I couldn't handle the shock of seeing another person I knew socially.

"You don't remember me, do you?"

I looked at his face, but there was nothing familiar about it. Just another perverted man about to fuck my waiting pussy and pump me full of cum.

"Last year? Parent teacher interviews? You taught my son, Eric."

I blinked in recognition. I vaguely remembered that meeting. So this was Eric's dad? He was a good kid. Dark if memory served, always scheming about something. I was about to get fucked by the dad of one of my former students. Could my day get any worse?

"I just want to say thanks for teaching my son," the man said.

I felt odd. "You're welcome, I guess."

"Now shut up and don't say a word. I'm going to drain my balls into that cute teacher cunt of yours, and there ain't anything you can do about it."

What a charming man. A woman, probably older than me, appeared at my side. I guessed she was his slave toy or possibly his wife. The woman idly grabbed my bare breast, and I looked at her with disdain. I felt Eric's dad force his cock into me, and I grunted. Shit, he was well endowed. I braced myself as the man grabbed my legs and started humping me without mercy.

* * *

When the last man had finished cumming inside my sore pussy, I was exhausted and thirsty. I was left on the table and ignored while the men who had all used me, gathered around a table to discuss the day's events.

Brittney snuck me a bottle of water and held it to my lips as I drank.

"Thank you," I whispered.

"They're voting now. I hope all this was worth it. How are you holding up?"

"I've been fucked more times today than in my entire life. How do you think I'm doing?"

Brittney laughed. "I don't know how you find the energy to crack jokes. I was totally worn out my first time here."

"Are you glad they accepted you?"

"Oh yeah," Brittney said. "I love this lifestyle. I'm sorry I had to suck on your pussy like that earlier. My Master cums a lot, but you get used to it."

I shook my head. "No, you were gentle. I liked it. All the women were gentle."

"I'm glad. I hope we can become friends. I like you more than the other slave girls here. Your Dom made a good choice in you."

"You said lifestyle earlier? It looked like you wanted to say more," I said. So long as I was stuck tied to a table, I thought I might as well chat with the only person in the room who treated me like a person.

Brittney looked over her shoulder at the men. No one was paying us any attention. She looked back at me and nodded. "This is a lifestyle. If you are accepted, like I was, then you become the communal property of all these men. It's a twenty-four seven commitment."

I frowned. "What do you mean twenty-four seven?"

"Parties, gatherings, private visits, birthdays, anniversaries, all of it. You are on call to service any one of these men any time of day or night. Once you two are voted in, I expect Brad to rekindle our old relationship. I can't wait to feel his cock in me again." Brittney said. She noticed my expression and blushed. "Oh, sorry. I forgot your feelings towards him. Don' be jealous, Julie. You aren't his first plaything nor the first girl he's tried to enroll with."

"I'm not?"

"Heavens no. Brad's done this twice before with other women. None of those relationships lasted, though. I hope that's different with you."

I glanced at Brad. His back was facing me. I suddenly wondered what kind of man I was involved with. He had never mentioned other women or trying to get back into the bondage club. Was I just a toy to him? Something to help further his selfish desires? Did he even love me?

"As soon as I get permission, I will undo these bindings. I bet you want a nice warm shower," Brittney said. "I did my first time."

"I hope I'm not pregnant. I've never had so much spunk in me before."

Brittney nodded. That concern was on her mind too it seemed. We waited in silence while the men debated and talked about my fate. Would I become a member of the club? Had I pleased them enough? I wasn't wild about this whole being on call thing. If what Brittney said was true, then any one of those men could request my presence for their kinky fulfillment? I had to talk that idea over with Brad first. I hadn't even known about the bondage club until all this started. I wasn't thrilled with the idea of being everyone's little whore despite the countless orgasm I had. I had to admit

I did enjoy myself. Intense would be the word to describe my experiences. I just hoped I wasn't pregnant now.

Brad walked over a little while later. He was smiling. Brittney watched silently. I peered at the face of the man I wasn't sure I loved anymore. Not after what he put me through. Our relationship would never be the same now.

"Have they voted?" I asked quietly.

"They have."

"Well?" I pressed.

"Welcome to the club."

I smiled weakly, but my heart sank. Britney helped untie me from the bench. My legs were weak, and my wrists and ankles were both chaffed red. There was no way I was going to be able to hide the marks from Tim when I got home.

That was the least of my worries, though. I had the accumulated semen of nine men in my fertile womb, and I was ovulating. Brad had picked the worst time of my cycle to offer me to the members of the club. Despite the best efforts of the nine accompanying woman to suck me clean, I knew there was still plenty more potent sperm still inside of me.

What if I became pregnant? How would I know who the father was? How would I explain it to my husband? Tim's vasectomy results had been verified. That's was why I never bothered going on the pill. Until today, I had never had intercourse with another man, and now, on my first mess-up I got plowed by nine cocks, and each and every one of them dumped their loads deep inside of me. In a morose sort of way, if you're going to fuck up then you may as well fuck up huge.

"I need to shower," I told Brittney as she offered me her shoulder for support. I looked at Brad, but he was talking and laughing with the other men. Even if he wanted to, Brad wouldn't help a submissive in front of those men. I was on my own.

Brittney only nodded and helped me off the stage and through the door back towards the change room. I desperately wanted more water, and also what time it was. When I entered the change room, Brittney helped pull my stiletto heels off, and roll down my white stockings. Too tired to care about the water temperature, I stumbled towards the shower stall, stepped inside and cranked both taps. The initial shock of cold water made me gasp and brought my mind to focus. I decided I liked the cold water; it numbed my body and sent shivers up my sides. Eventually, the warmth came, and I luxuriated under the powerful jet stream for a long time.

When I got out, Brittney was waiting with a towel which she wrapped around my shoulders. She handed me a smaller towel for my hair as well, and I thanked her. After a quick scrub of my wet hair with the towel, I smiled at Brittney who was holding an open bottle of water. We traded towel for water, and I drank deeply.

"Feeling better now?" Brittney asked.

"A million times," I said somberly. "My pussy aches, though. I think I got chaffing down there. I'm not used to so much sex or that many hard cocks."

"I envy you," Brittney said casually.

"You do? Why?"

"I've been fucked so many times that I don't even feel pleasure anymore. The only way I can climax is with a strong vibrator."

I had no idea. "Could that happen to me as well?"

"It depends on how many men use you," Brittney explained. "At first I loved all the sex I got, but after a while, with the same nine guys, I became numb to it. Not to offend you, but I'm looking forward to being used by Brad. At least he is somewhat handsome. Those other guys are all fat and flabby. I don't enjoy spreading my legs for them anymore."

"Then why do you do all this?" I asked. "I mean if it isn't fun?"

Brittney chuckled quietly. "I guess you get used to it. In all honesty, I wouldn't give any of those men out there the time of day in the real world if I wasn't bound to be their submissive. I guess I do it because I like the loss of control. Those men make me feel dirty, and I suppose it thrills me in a perverted way. I could never go back to vanilla sex."

I laughed. "I think we are very similar. I didn't know this bondage club existed until today. Before, when I was with Brad, he made me feel dirty, and I loved how he took away my decisions. I guess a part of me likes being a submissive."

"A lot of women secretly do, but not many are brave enough to try it."

"I agree," I said as I hung the towel on a hook. "If Brad had asked me ahead of time if I wanted a gangbang, I probably would have said no. Even though it has always been a huge fantasy of mine."

"You didn't enjoy it?" Brittney asked.

"Oh, I did. But this was all too much too quickly. I've never slept with another man other than my husband, not even Brad. Sure I gave blowjobs and other things, but never full bore sex. Tonight I lost my anal virginity and had nine men cum inside of me. I think that stretched my limits enough for one day."

I started to dress in my regular clothes, but Brittney put her hand on my arm.

"Not yet, you have to go back, in the nude, and thank each man and then take the Oath of the Submissive. Then it will be official," Brittney said.

"Oath of the Submissive?" I asked with a raised eyebrow. "You're serious?"

"Part of the club initiation. We all did it. Come on, I'll be right beside you."

I blew out a frustrated breath and tossed my bra back on the bench. Fine, I thought. More humiliation. I followed Brittney back into the hallway and through the door leading to the club's main room. I wasn't wild about being completely naked, but at least I was clean and showered. Besides, each of the men in the room had already fucked me, so I didn't see how there was any sense in worrying about being naked.

It felt strange approaching a group of men that just had intercourse with you. I could remember the feel of each of their cocks inside of me. I felt vulnerable as if my body had no more secrets and had been put on display like a common thing.

Other than Brad, not a single one of the men who had just fucked me were anything near handsome. I was used by a group of over-the-hill middle-aged men. My stomach churned. I was glad everyone had put clothes back on at least.

Why did I want to join this club and be submissive to these men? I could see why Brittney was looking forward to Brad's attention. A stab of jealousy made me ponder my feelings. Despite being upset at what Brad had asked me to do, I did still have feelings for him.

"Ah, gentlemen, our newest little submissive is washed and clean," Principal Rowe said as I approached the men with Brittney at my side. He was the head of the club, so it was only natural that he would be in charge of the next step.

I clasped my hands in front of my and lowered my head, partly because it was the standard submissive pose, but also to avert my eyes from the leering men and the reminder that each and every one of them had fucked me.

"Once we administer the oath there will be a few administrative points to clear up and then Dom will take you home," Rowe said.

"Yes, Sir," I said quietly.

As I waited, the men gathered in rows of chairs and took their seats, each of their submissive women kneeling beside them on the floor. Brad and Rowe remained at the front of the group. I didn't see Brittney.

"Approach your Dom," Rowe said as he turned towards me.

I stepped forward and stood, naked and alone in front of the two men. I knew my bare backside was in full view of those sitting, but I didn't care.

"We will begin," Rowe said. He took a laminated card out of his pocket.

I glanced at Brad who seemed beyond pleased. He winked at me, but otherwise ignored my presence. It almost felt like this was a pseudo wedding ceremony.

"What is your name?" Rowe read from the card.

I looked at my principal and bit back a sarcastic remark. "Julie Snow."

"Are you over the age of consent?"

I nodded. "Yes, Sir."

"What is your occupation?"

"School teacher."

"Who is your Dominant?"

"Brad."

Rowe turned towards Brad and said, "Is this your submissive?"

"Yes," he said.

Back to me. "Are you ready to swear the Oath of the Submissive?"

I suddenly felt silly and suppressed a giggle. The men around me took this far too seriously. Calming my face, I nodded solemnly. "Yes, Sir."

"Very well then. Kneel and read the oath aloud for all to hear," Rowe said as he stepped towards me and held out a parchment scroll.

Kneeling on the floor, I unrolled the paper and noted the intricate script. Someone spent a lot of time and effort making it. Looking up I waited for direction, but Rowe only nodded and gestured for me to read. I cleared my throat:

The Oath of the Submissive

I, Julie Snow, hereby swear to the tenants this oath and to my Dominant, Brad.
Allow me the strength to obey commands I cannot fathom.
Allow me the spirit to know Brad's needs.
Allow me the kindness to choke back retorts.
Allow me the serenity to serve Brad in peace.
Allow me the love to show Brad myself.
Allow me the tenderness to comfort Brad.
Allow me the light to show us the way.
Allow me the wisdom to be an asset to Brad.
Let me be able to show Brad each day my love for my service to Brad.
Let me open myself up to completely belong to Brad.
Let my eyes show Brad the same respect, as I sit at his side, or kneel at his feet.
Let me accept my punishment with the grace of a woman.
Let me learn my place and to please Brad, beyond myself.

Grant me the power to give myself to Brad completely.
Give me the strength to please us both.
Permit me to love myself, in loving Brad.
Allow me the peace of serving Brad.
For it is my greatest wish, my highest power To make his life complete.
Let me understand that my body is not my own
My wishes and desires come after the wishes and desires of men
This oath I do swear, in the presence of many witnesses.
I relinquish my freedom and my choice to the men of this society
And to my loving Dominant
This, I do swear

When I finished reading, I rolled the parchment scroll back up and handed it to Rowe. He seemed very pleased and then gestured for Brad to stand beside me. I was still on my knees and assumed that was where I was supposed to stay. No one had told me otherwise.

"I now pronounce you both members of the Bondage Club. You may present your submissive to those assembled," Rowe said.

Brad turned to face the men sitting before him, and I followed suit shuffling on my knees. I wondered if I decided on my own to suddenly stand, would the assembled men go into apoplectic shock? Despite kneeling naked beside Brad, I did feel a certain perverse sense of accomplishment. According to Brittney, it wasn't easy to be considered for membership or pass the initiation test, and yet I had done both. If only the club were filled with gorgeous men, I lamented, I could get used to this.

"Thank you for your votes gentleman, it means a lot to my submissive and me. I at this moment I freely give Julie to the members of the bondage club to use as they see fit and claim for myself the self-same rights and privileges towards your submissives," Brad said.

I peered up at him in shock, but he ignored me. His eyes were lingering on Brittney. I felt that familiar stab of jealousy and looked away. So I was to be freely given to the members of the club? Well, Brittney had mentioned that earlier back in the change room. I wasn't thrilled about the idea, but if this was the next step in my journey into the bondage lifestyle, then I had to put my qualms aside. Now that I was a member, what harm could there be in testing the waters for a few weeks? In a perverse way, I was looking forward to taking part in the next initiation and watching another woman endure what I had.

One by one the men rose from their seats and came forward to congratulate Brad. I remained kneeling and silently looked up like an obedient dog hoping for someone's attention.

"Congratulations buddy, very impressive display today," one of the men said to Brad. The man looked down at me and gazed at my bare breasts. He seemed to be waiting for something, but I didn't know what.

Brad tapped me with his foot, and I looked at him.

"This is where you thank each of the members for helping you discover your true purpose in life," Brad said.

I blinked and looked at both men in front of me. "What true purpose is that?"

The man gasped as if the answer should have been obvious to me. Brad frowned and shook his head.

"My apologies, she is still learning her place. Thank the man for using you, Julie. Thank him for helping you understand that your purpose in life if to submit to the desires of men."

I looked at the man once more. There was a line forming behind him, and I sighed. I didn't want a crowd. More humiliation. I swallowed hard.

"Thank you, sir, for using me. And thank you also for showing me my true purpose in life," I said even in a flat tone.

The man smiled and then nodded. I repeated the same mantra to each of the men as they congratulated Brad and then looked at me. My cheeks burned with the humiliation of thanking strangers for fucking me. Was I somehow supposed to be grateful that men I didn't know had free access to my most private of places? Was I supposed to cheer that any one of these strange men might have impregnated me? I only thanked them because Brad wanted me to do it.

When I had thanked the last man, Brad permitted me to stand. Rowe then led us to a table where I was given a smartphone. Perplexed, I glanced at Brad.

"Keep this with you at all times. There is a club scheduling program that all members can access on their phones. On your phone you will be able to see when a member has booked your services," Rowe said.

"Pardon?" I asked quietly, unsure I understood the meaning of his words.

Brad turned to me. "Every member can book a session with you or any of the other submissives here. It's first come, first, serve. For example, if Mr. Rowe wants a session on Wednesday, but another man also wants the same day, then whoever booked you first on the schedule has precedence."

"Like I'm an escort?" I assumed I didn't have any say in who booked me. I wasn't sure I was wild about their system or requirements. I could handle being submissive to Brad, but to any of the other men too? I needed time to process.

Rowe laughed. "No, escorts get paid. You will be doing this for free as part of your obligations to the club to maintain your memberships. Each submissive is the collective property of every member. There are no exceptions."

There was an app for this?

"Open your phone," Brad said.

I slid my finger across the screen and was prompted for a password. I looked up in dismay. "It's locked."

Rowe nodded. "That is for privacy. Your password is *GoldenGirl24*."

I glanced at Brad sharply, and he appeared sheepish. Had he given my chat handle to Rowe as my password? I wasn't impressed. Suppressing sharp words, I entered the password, and my phone was accessible.

"Oh, and you have a small data plan and free local calls," Rowe said. "I better not find any long distance charges or overages on the bill."

I nodded and looked at my screen. There was one program. I tapped the icon, and a scheduling calendar opened. I could see the names of all the submissives in the club, and all the contact numbers and names of the men. Neither Brad nor my name was on the list.

"We're not on the list," I said.

Rowe glanced at Brad.

"Proper decorum, slave," Brad said to me.

"I'm sorry, Sir."

"I haven't updated the program as you've only just joined," Rowe said. "As you can see, there are already dates booked for various submissives. You are to check this calendar daily, and are expected to arrange your personal life so you can make your appointments."

"I see," I said quietly, ignoring Brad's sharp stare. I didn't say 'sir' on purpose.

"Tap any random calendar date you see booked," Rowe said.

I tapped Brittney's name for this coming Friday. All the details of her session popped up, including the time and location of her session. It showed who booked her, and it showed that Brittney had viewed the request and accepted. There was even a small blurb describing any details such as required clothing.

"I see that Brittney had accepted the booking," I said. "Does that mean the submissive is permitted to cancel or refuse?"

Rowe nodded. "Your woman is very perceptive," he said to Brad. "Yes, and No. A submissive is permitted one refusal a month. If she is late or misses a booked session, then her Dom will be given demerit points. Don't worry about that part now, I'll explain more later."

I didn't have any pockets, due to being naked, so I closed the phone and held it in my palm. Despite my fantasy of not having control, I felt having a schedule and demerit points to be a little over the top. I didn't want to be at the beck and call of sex-starved middle-aged men. I didn't want to lose my joy of sex like Brittney had and be forced for the rest of my life to use a strong vibrator.

"Once again, congratulations Brad. Your little slut performed very well, and I look forward to booking a session with her soon," Rowe said snapping me out of my thoughts. I looked at my principal with barely contained disgust and smiled.

"Thank you, sir," Brad said. He then turned to me and hooked his arm through mine and quietly walked me towards the door. I didn't even get a chance to say goodbye to Brittney. We left when Brad decided. I recalled as I walked that Rowe never once thanked me. He thanked Brad instead. Not that I would have said he was welcome.

"So, you're going to fuck Brittney now?" I asked in a strong whisper once we were out of earshot of Rowe.

Brad recoiled and blinked. "What business is that of yours?"

"I guess you got what you wanted. Are you happy?"

"What's the matter with you?" Brad asked.

"Nothing, *Master*," I retorted. "Is there anything, *Master*, requires of a slave, or can slave leave now, *Master*?"

"You can go. See yourself out," Brad said. He turned and walked away.

I felt a rush of anger. He used me to get into the club. Sure I enjoyed most of it, but he never thought to ask if this was what I wanted. Now I had the semen of all those men inside of me threatening to get me pregnant and also marks all over my body. To top off my humiliation, I was now expected to carry a smartphone with me at all times so I won't miss a terribly important session with some man who wanted to fuck me again? I stormed back to the change room, got dressed and headed for the exit.

I half expected Brad to meet me at the door and apologize or at least give me a hug, but as I neared the Strip Club doors leading towards the parking lot, I looked over my shoulder, and he wasn't there. There was no way I was going back to beg his forgiveness. It was time to return to my family.

After climbing into my van, I shut the door and started the engine. It was difficult fighting the urge to cry. The enormity of what I had just gone through was suddenly sinking in. Not only was I having an affair behind my husband's back, but I practically abandoned my son also. How could I have done that? Let strangers fuck me? I went down this dark path so I could feel young again, not so I could abandon my family.

Why was I subjecting myself to these degrading humiliations? Because I wanted to know what I had missed out on as a good girl who followed the rules? I suddenly felt shame. I had let men I didn't find attractive have their way with me, and not only that, but I allowed them to pump me full of dangerous semen. I even let Brad deflower my ass in full view of men I found repulsive.

It became apparent that I needed to shape up. I couldn't be a submissive. Sure it was fun at one time, but now I had a smartphone with a damn schedule! These men were expecting to book me for more of their sexual pleasure. What kind of woman was I? I even blinded myself to Brad's true intentions. He just wanted in the club. I thought he loved me, but it was all a ruse.

I pulled out of the parking lot and drove home. Glancing in the rearview mirror, I could see my eyes were bloodshot from crying. It occurred to me that I was a horrible human being, a lousy unfaithful wife, and a terrible mother. When I thought about my son, I cried all over again.

By the time I pulled into my driveway, I had tried to get it together. I took deep breaths and calmed my nerves. I'd fucked up, and I knew it. I let the fantasy get out of hand. I should have let the fantasy stay a fantasy. I'm a wife and a mother and a school teacher. Women like me don't have gangbangs. It was time to be a responsible person. I had to start over. I could do this. I had to do it before it was too late to turn back.

I walked into my house and closed the door behind me.

"How was your trip?" Tim asked from the kitchen.

Oh god! Of all the times he had to come upstairs, this was it. I hadn't even thought he would notice I was home until after I showered and changed my clothes, and my puffy red eyes had cleared up.

"Hi, hon. How's monkey?" I asked in what I hoped was a cheery voice. I turned away and fussed with the pile of shoes by the door, pretending I was sorting them with my foot. I didn't want Tim to see my face.

"What happened to your wrist?"

I glanced up. My arm was leaning against the closet door, and my shirt sleeve had snaked up my arm revealing the rope burns from my bondage session. I pulled my arm down and cradled it.

"Oh, nothing just got a little injured. I'll be fine," I said over my shoulder.

Shit, Shit, Fuck!

I could hear Tim walking towards me. "What do you mean injured?"

I had to think fast. "Oh, on the zip line. I didn't have my harness done up correctly, and the nylon strap thing just chaffed me a little. It's nothing."

"Zip line?" Tim frowned and grabbed my two hands, and that's when he spotted my other red wrist. He then looked me in the eyes.

"We went to that wild adventure place north of here. I've never ridden a zip line before. It was fun. I'll be fine. I just need to shower and change and maybe we can all go out for dinner? I feel like Chinese."

Tim didn't say anything at first. He just looked at me, my hands still cradled in his own. "You hardly seem to be wearing the right clothing to be spending your day at an outdoor adventure park. Plus you're afraid of heights, Julie. And you're also shaking."

"Am I?"

"Are you sure you got this from riding a zip line?"

I nodded.

Tim dropped my hands, but his eyes said he didn't believe a word I said. He turned and walked away. "Chinese would be great. Have a shower. I'll get the little monster changed and dressed."

I watched as he disappeared into the living room. Holding my hands in front of my eyes I held them steady and examined them. They were in fact shaking. My nerves must have been shot. A quick shower, a change of clothes and then a nice family dinner would settle me. If only I could wash off my guilt and start fresh.

* * *

Monday morning found me once again getting my son ready for daycare, making lunches and getting to school on time. Tim was still sleeping. He hadn't come to bed until nearly four in the morning. I wondered if he suspected anything. He had been quiet for our family dinner at the Chinese restaurant on Saturday night. On Sunday he barely spoke a word to me and spent the day gaming. I didn't mind. It gave me time to catch up on my laundry and get prepped for my student's exams. With summer right around the corner, life at school gets pretty hectic with last minute things.

I dropped my son off and grabbed a herbal tea from the drive-thru and then made my way to the school. I spotted Brad's little red car with an empty spot beside it. I kept driving and parked along the fence instead.

When I walked into the English Office, Brad was photocopying exams. He looked up when I walked in, but he didn't smile. His eyes almost seemed cold. I nodded to him briefly and set my things on my desk. I glanced at my cubbyhole mailbox. There were a few papers in it, so I walked over and snatched them.

"How are you feeling today?" Brad said.

I turned. "I'm sore. And I feel sick."

"Too much excitement over the weekend?"

"I think my husband suspects," I blurted and then clamped my mouth shut. I hadn't meant to reveal my thoughts, but they just tumbled out.

"What do you mean?" Brad asked. Another teacher had walked into the room, and he lowered his voice and stepped closer to me.

"He asked about the red marks on my wrists."

"What did you tell him?"

"I said I got hurt on the zip line. I had to make something up." I held up both my arms and pulled my long sleeve sweater down. "This is why you should have asked me before making me go through all that. Your friends left marks on me. What did you think would happen, Brad? You think no one was going to notice?"

"It's not my concern. Why didn't you cover your wrists?"

"Cover them? Really? How about why did you put me through that without even asking?"

"You loved it."

"That's beside the point. You should have asked me first."

The other teacher was looking at us. I turned away, my fac red, and cursed. I hadn't meant to say what I had so loud. I could imagine the teacher wondering why Brad and I were fighting. The only solace is if the teacher went to the principal, it would be ironic. I nearly laughed at the ludicrousy of it all. I could imagine the teacher running to Principal Rowe and telling him that I had strange red marks on my wrists. Well no guff, Rowe would say. I put them there.

When I turned to see if the teacher was still listening, he had already left. Brad was thinking. He turned to me.

"What?" I said in a defensive tone. I was ready to fight.

"I'm sorry."

I blinked. "Pardon?"

"I said, I'm sorry. You were right. I should have consulted with you first. It was wrong of me just to assume you would want to do it. Can you forgive me?"

His apology took the wind out of my sails. But I still had a little puff left. "Brad, what those men did to me hurt. I could have gotten pregnant. Look, I love what we do together, but joining that club, is just too much. I'm not sure I'm ready for that kind of lifestyle. I have to think about my husband and son."

He nodded and put his arm around me.

It felt nice to have my feelings acknowledged. At least he finally knew what a mistake it had been. Perhaps we could go back to a less crazy kind of bondage lifestyle. One that didn't involve gang bangs or anal sex.

"Forgive me, pumpkin?"

I couldn't help but grin. I was still upset, but I smiled. "I forgive you."

"Okay then. Well, I need to tidy this mess up and get to class. I take it you didn't get much exam prep done on the weekend?" Brad asked.

"No, I didn't get much prep done. I was a little tied up," I said as I grabbed my lesson plans and walked out of the office. I was tempted to look at Brad's expression, but I didn't need to look back to know what was on his face.

As my morning progressed, I had time to deal with my mixed emotions over my wild weekend. One thing I had to be careful about was keeping my wrists hidden from the prying eyes of the students and faculty. My skin was healing, but the red rope burns were still visible. Just before the lunch bell rang, I was notified that Principal Rowe needed to see me in his office right away.

I felt my heart skip a beat when I heard his name. What could the head of the bondage club want with me? A sense of dread settled over me as I walked to his office. Did he have some nefarious plans for me? I doubted he just wanted to chat.

When I arrived at the office, the secretary smiled and pointed towards the principal's door and told me the others were already there. *Others?*

When I opened Rowe's door, I felt my face flush. Brad and Jennifer were already there, and they looked at me as I closed the door behind me and glanced at Principal Rowe.

"It's so good to see you, Julie," Rowe said. "Please have a seat."

"What is this about?" I asked, choosing to stand.

"Just an informal meeting. Please, could you be a dear and lock that door. Thank you," Rowe said.

I locked the door, feeling my stomach tense as I did so. Brad stood and walked over to Rowe. The two men smiled and glanced at Jennifer and me. Standing next to the door, with my hands clasped in front of me, I watched nervously. Jennifer got out of her chair and sauntered over to Brad. My eyes followed her. I gasped in shock as she wrapped her arms around Brad's shoulders and started to kiss him. Brad ran his hands up and down her back and then fondled her ass through her skirt. Rowe looked at me. *What was going on?*

There was no way I was kissing my principal. First of all, kissing was too intimate, and secondly, I didn't find him attractive in the least, and besides, I was quitting the bondage club, so I wasn't obligated to whore myself to anyone. Rowe shrugged and turned his attention back to Brad and Jennifer as did I.

For a moment I felt like I was in a dream. Brad was brazenly kissing Jennifer in front of me. They even waited until I was in the office to start. Was this supposed to be another test or teaching moment where my boundaries were once again stretched? Was he trying to make me jealous? Well, it wasn't working.

I folded my arms and looked at Brad in disgust. Despite what he said earlier, it was clear by his actions that our relationship meant nothing more to him than a way to satisfy his cock. There was no exclusivity.

How ironic, that I had cheated on my husband with a man who was now cheating on me. Not that we were dating or anything, but I had thought what we had was special. Did Brad think I was going to stand in the principal's office and watch him make out with another teacher and do nothing? I turned to leave.

"Stay there," Rowe said, his voice stopping me. He held up his hand.

"Why? I don't want to watch this. If he wants to kiss another woman, fine."

"I want you to watch," Rowe said. He patted the side of the desk he was leaning against. "Come, stand here beside me."

I did what he asked, leaning against his large wooden desk. Rowe put his arm around my shoulder, and I resisted the urge to brush it off. That would have been rude. Despite being the head of the bondage club, Principal Rowe was still my boss. If I wanted to have my teaching contract renewed then, I had to play nice.

"You aren't looking at them," Rowe observed. "I want you to watch."

Fine, I'll watch. I crossed my arms and looked at Brad as his hands groped Jennifer's ass. She was younger than I was and despite not caring, I felt a stab of jealousy. He thought she

192

was prettier and me. Jennifer was responding to his kissing with obvious excitement. She ran her hands up and down his torso, and then over the bulge in his pants.

"Would you like to suck me off?" Brad asked Jennifer. His eyes quickly glanced at me, and he smirked.

"Yes, if Master will allow it," Jennifer said in a seductive tone. She glanced at Rowe for approval. He nodded and Jennifer clapped her hands in excitement and quickly got on her knees.

I felt disgusted. Brad made eye contact with me again as Jennifer tore open his pants and pulled out his hard cock. I wondered what he was thinking. I could see and hear Jennifer eagerly working his cock in her mouth. My lips became a thin line. He was showing me that he could have sex with other women and that I didn't own him. Our relationship wasn't going to be monogamous. It also wasn't going to last. He was sealing his doom and didn't even know it.

Two can play at this game. I raised an eyebrow at Brad and then turned my attention to Principal Rowe and gently rubbed the bulge in his pants. Rowe gasped and looked at me. I smiled, bit my lip and continued to rub his crotch gently.

"Would you like me to suck you off, Principal Rowe?" I asked quietly.

He glanced at Brad for the barest of moments and then returned his gaze to me. Nodding quickly, he began to undo his pants. I guessed he wanted to be quick in case I changed my mind.

"Oh no, sir," I said, brushing his hands aside. "Let Slave do that. You just relax. An important big man like you needs a woman to do the work."

Rowe leaned back and braced his arms on his desk while I pulled down his zipper and undid the belt on his slacks. I fished his hard cock out of his boxers and gingerly stroked it. My stomach wanted to revolt as I looked at his fifty-something-year-old cock. Principal Rowe was more than twice my age, but that didn't matter right now. Brad thought it was fine to have his dick sucked in front of me; then I wanted to suck another man's cock in front of him.

I knelt on the floor of the office and opened my mouth. Rowe was already hard and ready to be sucked, but I needed a few moments to build my courage. The sound of Jennifer slurping on Brad's dick angered me. I wolfed down Rowe's cock like my life depended on it. I wanted to show Brad what he was missing. I could suck a cock better than that tart Jennifer, and I was going to demonstrate it to everyone.

Rowe's cock tasted salty and musky, but I ignored the less than savory flavor and did my best to remain enthusiastic. I stroked and sucked, and quickly found a rhythm I could maintain almost indefinitely. Rowe stared at me while I sucked him off. I didn't care for his creepy expression, but I smiled anyway, ignoring the thought that he was old enough to be my father. His cock hit the back of my mouth and my eyes watered, and I gagged a little, but I refused to slow.

Relax your throat, I told myself, as I prepared to give Row something Brad had never experienced with me. Moving my hands to the sides of Rowe's hips, I gripped firmly and then pulled my head and torso into him. I felt his cock hit the back of my mouth, and despite my best efforts, I made gagging sounds. I ignored my urge to retch and continued to force the thick shaft down my throat. My eyes sprung tears as I pulled my body closer and his cock slipped in deeper and deeper.

Finally, my nose touched Rowe's thick unkempt pubic hair, and I stopped. Holding my breath, I moved my head back and forth letting him enjoy a little throat fuck.

My stamina was limited, though, and I pulled my head back, but I suddenly felt his hands grabbing the back of my head and stopping me. I shuffled my knees and looked up at Rowe's face with wide eyes. I had to blink tears away to focus on his face, and when I saw clearly, he was grinning at me.

"Keep it there for as long as you can," Rowe said. "Can you do that?"

I nodded, feeling my panic subside. My face became red as I tried to relax and hold my breath. Without consciously forcing myself to relax, I could see how a person could easily begin to panic. Rowe's grip on my head was iron-like, and he gave his nearly buried cock a few short thrusts back and forth. My eyes brimmed and then overflowed, and my face must have changed from red to a darker shade. I couldn't hold my breath much longer. I pushed on his hips with my hands and Rowe released his grip. I pulled back, feeling his cock snake up my throat and out of my mouth. I gasped and sucked in large quantities of air as my color returned to normal. Gobs of saliva trailed down my chin and hung like streamers.

"Very good," Rowe said. "Now do it again."

I glanced at Brad. He was watching me with lust in his eyes and completely ignoring Jennifer's attention to his cock. I gave him a satisfied nod and returned to Rowe's glistening hard cock. Taking a few deep breaths, I slipped his cock back into my mouth, past my gag reflex and down my throat. Part of me felt dirty and whorish, but another part of me was proud that in just a few short months, I had gone from terrible at blowjobs to fully deepthroating.

"Will you swallow my cum?" Rowe asked me.

I was somewhat appreciative that he bothered to ask, so I nodded while looking out of the corner of my eye at Brad. He was still watching me. Perhaps the sight of his submissive with a man's cock fully down her throat turned him on. I didn't care. I just wanted him to see what he wasn't going ever to get from me again.

Once more Rowe gripped my head in his hands and held it steady, but this time, he pulled back and then rammed his cock forward. The sensations were strange, and I sucked air through my nose as best I could while staying relaxed.

He humped my face even harder. I didn't enjoy his rough treatment of me, but I knew he would finish soon, so I endured the humiliation. He buried his cock and then made a series of short in and out thrusts before gasping and grunting and pulling my nose into his pubic hair and mashing it. I pushed on his legs with my arms, but he held me firm. Then his cock began to pump. I could feel it first with my tongue. I held very still. I had never had a man cum in my throat, and I wondered if it would get into my lungs or something.

I tried to breathe, but all I got was a nose full of his musky odor. His cock spurted and convulsed as his balls drained. I swallowed and gulped and waited for him to finish, but I was running out of air. My face was beyond red once more, and my eyes streamed tears. I suddenly remembered I wasn't wearing waterproof mascara. I knew my cheeks would be streaked with black lines.

Damnit!

When his orgasm was over, and he released my head, I pushed against him hard and got his cock out of my throat as fast as I could. I gasped and gulped air and swallowed. His orgasm felt weird. I hadn't tasted any of it.

"Oh my god, did you just cum down my throat?"

"Is that a problem?" Rowe asked. He gestured towards his spent cock.

I remembered the rule about cleaning a man after sucking him off, but I had half a mind to refuse him. Then I remembered that Brad was watching. I ignored my revulsion and slipped his cock back into my mouth. I formed a seal with my lips and made long pulls deliberate pulls with my mouth. I knew that would entice Brad. I could taste Rowe's sperm, and though I found it revolting, I swallowed and licked my lips as if his cum was the best I had ever tasted. Anything to twist that knife just a little deeper, I thought. When I was finished licking my lips, I watched as Rowe tucked his clean cock away, and then I glanced up at his face and smiled.

"Thank you, Sir," I said in my most innocent voice.

Rowe had turned to glance at Jennifer. She was still sucking Brad's cock, having failed to bring him to orgasm as quickly as I had brought Rowe. I smiled triumphantly at Brad, pleased that his little tart wasn't as practiced as I was.

Brad gripped the top of Jennifer's head and held her steady. With his other hand, he pulled his cock from her mouth and started jerking off, never once taking his eyes off of my face. I raised an eyebrow, fascinated at his intense expression. His face contorted, and he began to spurt his cum all over Jennifer's face and hair. He didn't even look at her, he just locked eyes with me and let his cum splatter where it may. I could hear Jennifer gasp and cry in surprise as she lifted her hands and shook them, fingers spread wide in a helpless gesture.

When he was done, Brad brought her head forward and slipped his cock into her mouth. He grabbed handfuls of her hair and forced her head back and forth, cleaning his cock without care. I watched the back of Jennifer's head bob back and forth as she cleaned his shaft. Then Brad stepped back and yanked up his pants. Jennifer leaned to her side and caught her breath. Her hands gently touched her cum glazed face.

"Thank you," Jennifer said quietly, though it didn't sound like she meant it.

I spotted a water cooler in the corner of Mr. Rowe's office and was tempted to rinse the salty aftertaste from my mouth. Instead, I looked at Brad. I wanted to see the expression on his face. Was he jealous I had performed oral on the principal? It seemed he was bothered, and I smiled inwardly.

"I have to congratulate you, Brad, on the quality of Julie's cock sucking skills. I enjoyed her. I might even go so far and say she is better than your ex-wife was. Mind you, your ex always serviced me well, but Julie here has more spirit and enthusiasm. I have to commend you," Rowe said.

Brad nodded.

"What do you mean his ex-wife?" I asked, looking at Rowe. "I didn't know he was divorced." I swiveled my eyes towards Brad. "Is this true?"

Brad shrugged. "We split last year."

I gasped. "All this time, I thought you had a wife. You mean to tell me you're not married? Wait a minute. What about all those times you couldn't chat with me, or you said you had to go because your wife was cranky?"

"I'm separated."

"So you were lying to me. Why pretend unless–" I stopped. A thought entered my mind, and my eyes narrowed. It all made sense now. I was a fool not to see it before. Brad was acting like a single man the entire time. No wonder we never went to his place, he didn't want me to know he lived alone.

"You've been playing the field," I said.

Jennifer laughed.

I looked at her. She looked ridiculous covered in Brad's sum. "What?"

"Brad's ex-wife was his first submissive pet. She tried it for a while, but couldn't keep up with the demands. They fought, and she left. Poor little Julie, did you think Brad was only just tapping that sweet little ass of yours?"

My face flushed, and I felt like slapping that haughty look on her face.

"You've met Brittney haven't you?" Jennifer continued.

My mouth dropped open, and I looked at Brad. His face told me everything I needed to know. "You've been sleeping with Brittney all this time?"

"And me," Jennifer said with an annoying giggle. "Sometimes I sucked him off while you two lovebirds chatted online. Oh, what fun those days were!"

"Is this true?" I asked.

Brad held still for a moment and then nodded. "Yes. When I got tired of your whining and pestering and endless questions, and I needed some release I slept with Brittney and Jennifer."

I felt my lip tremble. "So you used me. You lied to me, and you used me."

"No dear, he was grooming you to be his next submissive," Jennifer said in a mocking tone. "I got tired of hearing about it. We all did. But he was making progress, so we were patient. You see, Brittney and I are spoken for by other men. You, on the other hand, were fresh and available. He needed you to get into the bondage club, and you did an admirable job," Jennifer said.

"Enough," Rowe said. "Take your squabbles elsewhere. You two ladies use my private washroom and clean up. Classes start soon."

"No," I said.

"Pardon?" Rowe asked, his face startled. He wasn't used to that word.

"I'm done. I'm not your pet anymore Brad, and I'm not degrading myself sucking off men old enough to be my father just to win you back. I see what you are now. You used me, but I let you. It's my fault too, but this ends now."

Brad looked at Rowe.

"I think you should reconsider, young lady," Rowe said casually. Too casually. I looked at him and felt a chill at the confidence on his face.

"Why should I?"

Rowe walked around his desk and opened a drawer. He removed a stack of CD's and placed them in front of him.

"Let's see," he said while picking up the first disk. "Ahh, this is a nice one. The complete collection of text messages between you and Brad." He dropped that disk and picked up another. "This one is a collection of nude photos you emailed him. I have a copy of this at home. Great spank material."

"Stop!" I said, but he ignored me. He had to be lying.

"Here are recorded video chats. This disk is from the bondage club. Oh, your first anal with Brad. I might copy this one. I have each man who fucked you labeled by name. Shall I continue?"

"You are blackmailing me," I said. Brad was smiling, and Jennifer was beside herself with glee.

"I think we have an understanding. Imagine a copy finding its way into your husband's hands. Think of the damage to your marriage. Think of your husband filing for divorce and getting custody of your son."

"You leave my son out of this!" I said fiercely.

"Where mysterious copies of these end up is of course, entirely up to you. You can leave. You can even leave Brad and your duties to the bondage club. That choice is yours. Imagine the consequences of these disks falling into the wrong hands. Posted on the internet even. I wouldn't take long for some student to recognize his teacher and then oops the board office finds out, and suddenly you're divorced and fired from ever teaching again, but also shunned. By all means, leave. But there is another option."

I felt trapped. It had never occurred to me that Brad would have recorded all our private messages and video. I certainly had no idea they had filmed me during my initiation at the bondage club.

He was right, though. If my husband found out, I would lose everything. If the school board found out, I would be fired. Without a teaching job, his lawyer would shred me in court. Probably produce humiliating evidence and make it all public. The judge would rule in his favor, and I would lose my son.

"Would you like to reconsider your rash statement, Julie?" Rowe asked.

Brad was looking at me. I wanted to scream at him for betraying me. My mind raced, but I could see no other option. All the evidence they had on me, was things I did willingly. I ruined my marriage by going down this dark path. I wanted fun and adventure, but I got used. Now I was trapped. I hung my head and clasped my hands in front of me.

"I've changed my mind," I said quietly.

"You will stay Brad's submissive?" Rowe asked.

I nodded as tears rolled down my face. I was truly trapped.

"I can't hear you."

"Yes, sir. I understand," I said.

"Good. You see, a woman just needs a strong man to help keep them in line, and sometimes remind them of their purpose in life. Your purpose is to serve Brad, and by extension, the members of the bondage club. Now I think Brad deserves an apology," Rowe said.

I sniffled as more tears rolled down my cheek. I finally understood that Brad had never loved me. He pretended he did. I was such a fool. Taking a deep breath, I felt the weight of my poor decisions crushing my spirit.

"I'm sorry for speaking so rashly," I said.

"You can make it up to me later. I think I'll fuck you after school today. Meet me here after the last bell. Thank god I don't have to pretend to give a shit about you anymore. I think a suitable punishment would be to make you my anal slave for the next few months," Brad said. "Would you like that?"

"Whatever Master wishes," I said.

Jennifer giggled. I stared at the floor in shame. All my anger had dissolved and was replaced with guilt. I felt like a prisoner in front of a judge and jury that just heard the sentence given. Life in prison, with no possibility of parole. I had to accept my fate. I had done all this to myself. I felt sick to my stomach. I was simply a submissive slave now and nothing more. I had finally discovered what was at the end of my journey down the dark path I so willingly traveled:

Enslavement.

The End

THE JJ STUART CATALOGUE
Jake & Robin: The Wife Slave Series

Decided
Broken.
Revenged
Also available as a complete Trilogy

Katie's Mom Series

Watching Katie's Mom
Caught by Katie's Mom
Punished by Katie's Mom
Shared by Katie's Mom
Also available as a complete Series

Down the Dark Path Trilogy

A Cheating Wife's Journey from Innocence to Submission

Book 1. The Fall of Julie Snow
Book 2. The Training of Julie Snow
Book 3. The Demise of Julie Snow
Also available as a complete Trilogy

My Wife The Kinky Escort

Book 1. Hired By Her CO-Worker
Book 2. Rite of Passage

Stand Alone Sizzling Quick Reads

The Dominant Wife: Femdom, male chastity cuckold!

Love on the Beach: A secret rendezvous leads to a torrid love affair with a hot wife!

A Romp in the Gym: A late night encounter with an ex might solve her fertility problems!

Tara's First Time Tied: Can she handle her first BDSM sex with her secret lover?

Thank you for all your support and feedback. Feel free to send me an email or sign up for my discreet mailing list, or if you have story ideas you would like to suggest and see in print, drop me a line. I'd be glad to hear from you!

J.J.Stuart@hotmail.com

Printed in Great Britain
by Amazon

29024456R00116